Soleil

By Lainie Suzanne

Soleil

Find out more about the author and upcoming books online
at www.lainiesuzanne.com

SOLEIL
ISBN-13:978-0692333532
SOJO Publishing
Cover Artist: Lainie Suzanne
Published in the United States of America

This book is a work of fiction. Names, characters, places, and incidents either are products of the author's imagination or are used fictitiously. Any resemblance to actual persons, living or dead, events, or locales is entirely coincidental.

Disclaimer: Adult Content – The Material in this book is for mature audiences only and contain graphic sexual content. It is intended only for those aged 18 and older.

Soleil

Acknowledgements

To my Husband, the Love of my Life – Thank you for all of your unwavering love and support.

I couldn't do this without you. I love you!!!

To my Children – You are 4 amazing people that I'm honored to call mine.

I love you!

To my family and friends – Thank you for your love, friendship, and support!

To my Street Team ~ Lainie's Nexus Naughties ~

You ladies ROCK!!! Thank you for all you do for me!!!

I'm blessed to have you on my *Team*.

TABLE OF CONTENTS

CHAPTER 1	**5**
CHAPTER 2	**13**
CHAPTER 3	**25**
CHAPTER 4	**35**
CHAPTER 5	**44**
CHAPTER 6	**53**
CHAPTER 7	**64**
CHAPTER 8	**73**
CHAPTER 9	**84**
CHAPTER 10	**91**
CHAPTER 11	**103**
CHAPTER 12	**115**
CHAPTER 13	**128**
CHAPTER 14	**139**
CHAPTER 15	**153**
CHAPTER16	**163**
CHAPTER 17	**175**
CHAPTER 18	**190**

CHAPTER 1

What to wear...what to wear??? I hate going on blind dates. I know it's not really a blind date. I've seen him, talked to him. Well, I guess you can call it talking. But this is face to face; on my own to come up with conversation. *What if we really have nothing in common? Reminder to self: steer clear of religion and politics.*

I don't want to dress too sexy. He'll think I'm easy and desperate. I don't want to dress too conservative. He'll think I'm a stuffy, boring prude. It's supposed to be casual dress; just dinner at a local pub. *So what are you stressing about? It's just a date.*

I'm sticking with the original outfit I planned; coral button down shirt dress, belted; with leggings, boots, and hopefully Kathy's beautiful floral scarf that matches this shirt perfectly.

"Deb..." Kathy's voice calls out through the apartment.

"Back here."

"What the hell are you doing leaving your front door

unlocked? You obviously couldn't hear me knocking, so you wouldn't hear an intruder either. I tried the doorknob and the door opened. That is so dangerous!" She scolds me.

Kathy's been through a lot the past 6 months, between the home invasion and being attacked in her hotel room while on a business trip. Both at the hands of that psycho co-worker that had been stalking her. She's a little on edge about safety and rightfully so. My best friend for over 20 years, she's the sister I never had.

"You're right, Kathy. I should've been more careful. I carried in groceries earlier and forgot to go back and lock the door. Stupid move on my part."

"I just don't want anything to happen to you. Anyways...here's the scarf. What did you decide to wear?"

"This..." I motion my hand toward the ensemble spread across my bed.

"Ooooo... the scarf does match perfectly with the coral color. You'll look fab-u-lous,"Kathy enunciates each syllable of the word.

"Thanks, hun!"

"Are you sure you wanna do this? I mean, go out on this date. Are you sure?" Kathy asks, concern lacing her words.

"I'm a little nervous, but I think it will be okay. Hopefully, we'll have some common interests. And hopefully, he's not a serial killer."

"Not funny..." Kathy snips. "There are some real creepers on these dating sites. You have to be cautious."

"I know...I'm trying to be as cautious as possible. I've chatted with him on video, so I have an idea of what he looks like for real, so I won't be fooled that way. I'm meeting him at the restaurant so he doesn't know where I live. Trying to keep it safe," I explain.

"That's smart of you, Deb."

"Hey, we're meeting at 7:30pm, so will you call me around nine o'clock to be my escape, if need be?"

"Sure... So, will I be sick, have a flat tire, car won't start?" She asks excitedly.

"Hmmm...Let's go with your car won't start," I snicker.

"All righty..."

"Good, I feel better already," I let out a long sigh.

"So...have you thought anymore about coming to Nexus? I know you have a freakin' serious attraction to Patrick," Kathy swoons.

"Umm...No Patrick. He's so fucking HOT...I can't think when I'm near him. Besides, I remember all the women drooling and nearly humping his leg at the cookout at Nexus, Labor Day weekend. See, I went to that Nexus event."

I would've been dry humping his leg too, if I could've gotten close enough to him. Those women were swarming his sexy ass. Tall with dark walnut hair that looks like he ran his fingers through it to style; soft amber eyes, a dark shadow outlining his strong jaw line and surrounding his delectable plump mouth. A shiver dives down my spine recalling his six feet of decadence.

"Technically, it was a cookout at Isaac's but he invited a lot of the members from the club," she replies. "Women do literally fall at his feet offering their 'submission' to him and he does play with some of them, but nothing serious. I've seen the way he looks at you, Deb. I really think he's interested in you."

"WHAT?!?! Do you seriously believe that, Kathy?"

She stares at me dumbfounded..."Yeah, I do. I've seen it with my own eyes."

"Patrick is that guy who looks at every woman like she's the most beautiful creature in the world. He has that old world, chivalrous air about him. It's not directed just at me. He was that way with all the women at the cookout; married or not. That's just his personality," I explain, shrugging my shoulders.

"Oh...O-kay," Kathy rolls her eyes.

"Look...I have to focus on this date tonight, not a dream."

"Suit yourself...I gotta run, though. Isaac will be late getting home today and Patrick is working too, so I have to open the club tonight. I'll give you a call around nine, to check in on ya."

"Thanks chickie..." I reply hugging her neck. "Hey...lock the door, please!" I yell down the hall at Kathy's back.

****

Patience is not one of my virtues, so I'm getting antsy. Checking my watch to see how much time has lapsed since the last time I checked. Hmm, two minutes. I check my phone...no missed calls. The pub is pretty busy, but not loud. I left my name and his name with the hostess, so he could easily find me. I'm struggling not to finish my glass of wine before he gets here. It's 7:48. I'm giving him until 8 o'clock to show; then I'm leaving. I'm not a stickler for punctuality, but I am for manners and courtesy. *I HATE blind dates.*

My gaze pans across pub. I'm positioned where I can see the front door, the hostess stand, and most of the bar. My eyes pivot around the room once more and my target appears in the crosshairs. Beaming a smile that shows he doesn't have a care or concern in the world, the sandy-haired hottie, the same age as me, *why do men age so much better than women,* struts across the floor towards me. *Does he not care that he's almost 30 minutes late!*

"Hey gorgeous, I'm Kevin." His introduction oozes from his mouth, while pulling the chair out and sitting. He snatches up the menu, then quickly puts it back down and raises his hand, snapping his fingers to get the waitress' attention.

I sit, speechless, waiting for an explanation to his tardiness, which I don't believe is coming. I peer at my watch again, to see if that will provoke a response. *Mmm...Nope.* The waitress comes over silencing his persistent finger-snapping.

"Hey gorgeous, whatcha got on tap?" *Again with the gorgeous.* Giggling, the young waitress recites the list of beers. His salutation has a far better effect on her than me.

He orders some type micro-brew and I order another glass of Zinfandel. She turns to walk away from the table and his head turns too; focusing on the waitress's ass shaking from side to side, barely covered by her skirt. *He's not even trying to be inconspicuous about it.*

Shaking my head, I try to rid myself of the contempt flowing through my veins and adjust my attitude.

"So... did you have car trouble?" I politely ask.

"Huh, what?"

"Car trouble. Did you have car trouble? Is that why you were late?" I repeat my question, expanding my thought for clarity.

"I drive a 2013 Tesla Roadster."

"Nice. Did it break down?"

"Do you even know what a Tesla Roadster is? It costs $90,000" his words drenched in condescension.

"Umm, It's...a *car*. So, did your $90,000 car break down?" My words prickle with disdain.

"No, gorgeous... it didn't break down," he chuckles sarcastically. *Again with the gorgeous...*

I just stare at him, waiting for an explanation. I wouldn't normally react this way, but his smug and shmarmy attitude has flipped my bitch switch.

"I was in the middle of something and couldn't get away," he smirks.

Trying to salvage at least the meal, I take a cleansing breath to tamper down my temper and change the subject. "I recall from our talks that you're in real estate, is that right?"

"You got it. I won the Best of Atlanta Real Estate Award, residential division, two years ago. My sales shot through the roof. Guess everybody wants to be handled by the best," he winks.

"Uh, huh..."

The waitress returns with our drinks, carefully sitting my wine in front of me. She turns toward Kevin, bending over far enough for her blouse to fall away from her chest, exposing her breasts openly.

Not just sneaking a peek, as most men would, Kevin blatantly ogles the sight before him, "Nice view."

The two pass overtly sexual looks between them, like I'm not sitting here. The waitress walks away as I pilfer through my purse for my keys.

"Hey gorgeous...going somewhere?"

"Gorgeous, huh??? Do you know my name? We've spoken several times on the phone and on skype. So... do you know my name?" I quip.

"Uh..."

"Didn't think so..."

Standing, I grab my purse and keys and walk around the table. He grabs my wrist, as I scoot between him and the person at the table beside him.

"Where are you going? The night's just getting started."

I glare down at him, "You're an egotistical twat and I'm not wasting another minute on you." Wrenching my wrist out of his grasp, I storm out.

CHAPTER 2

Who the hell does he think he is? Obviously...God's gift to women and all mankind. Pompous ass! Such a waste of my time. As soon as I get home, I'm canceling my subscription to that dumbass dating site. I'm not going through this bullshit anymore. The chirping of my phone halts my mental rant about the night.

"Hey Kathy..."

"Hey, escape trap calling. How's it going?"

"Not so good...I'm heading home."

"Home??? Already??? It's only 9 o'clock. What happened?"

"He was a prick, so I left. I'm sure he'll find his way home with the waitress."

"The waitress?"

"Yeah, he was more interested in her than...well, he was mostly interested in himself."

"Aawww... Deb, I'm sorry."

"Don't be. Live and learn...I'm heading home to curl up with a good book and a glass of wine."

"Okay, drive safe. I'll talk to you tomorrow."

"Okay."

****

My Sunday routine...I normally love the drive down to Macon to see my parents, but today I don't want to reach my destination. I'd rather keep driving and driving. The finality of it all will slap me in the face when I get there. Dad's health has deteriorated to the point that Hospice has been called in.

It's not that I didn't know this day was coming. I did. The prognosis was that Dad would only live a few months. Once symptoms present themselves, it's usually too late; the viciousness of Pancreatic Cancer. Such a painful disease, but this cancer didn't know how strong my dad is or was; he's lived a year and a half since his diagnosis. However, it's taken its toll on him and Mom.

Vincent Leon Giroux, born in France and immigrated to America with his parents when he was a small child after World War II. He fought in Vietnam until an explosion took the sight from his left eye. He returned home and married his high school sweetheart, Mary. A year later they had their only child... Debra Leònne Giroux.

Though he has lived here in the Deep South most of his life, he still has his beautiful accent. Unfortunately, I didn't pick up his accent, nor the beautiful language. I know a few of the basics, like most people, but that's it. I didn't even take French in school. Such a slacker... But I will always cherish the phrase my dad always greets me with... *Ma Belle Fille - My Beautiful Daughter.*

He looks so frail, lost so much weight. His hand rests in mine while I trace the veins raised in his hand. Caressing with each stroke, I outline the features of his face with my finger.

"Daddy...it's me, Debra. I'm here daddy," tears welling in my eyes.

The nurse said he's in a deep sleep, not a coma. She said to talk to him, because he can hear us. Mom said he's been unresponsive all day. I know it's only a matter of time. The nurse said it could be anytime or he could linger for weeks. It makes it difficult living two hours away. I want to stay and be here for Mom, but I have to work. Sure I can take time off, but I could use up all my leave if he continues fighting. Then, when he does pass and mom needs me here, I wouldn't have any leave left. *God, I feel so torn...*

"Ma b-belle fille..." A broken whisper floats to my ears. His hand moves in an attempt to squeeze mine, but it's only a flutter because he's so weak.

"Oh Daddy...I'm here."

He opens his eyes to me, though they are void of recollection.

He struggles to see me, even though I'm right beside him. It's like he's looking past me. I've always heard that sometimes you need to tell those on the verge of dying, that it's okay for them to go, to let them know you'll be okay.

"Daddy, I love you so very much. You've fought so hard. I want you to know we're okay. I will take care of Mom, I promise," whispering in his ear.

He tries again to squeeze my hand and closes his eyes.

Upon Mom's promise to call if anything changes, I reluctantly head back home. Tears flow from my eyes for the entire drive. It's cathartic for me, as I realize that was probably the last time I'll ever see my dad.

****

Tossing and turning all night, I feel like crap this morning. Though I'm emotionally drained, I know work is the best thing for me right now. It'll help keep my mind off of Dad. Monday mornings are usually busy at the bank, for one reason or another and today's no exception. Stepping out of my office, I call the name of the next person waiting.

"Mr. Moore..." I softly call out to the reception area where two men and one woman are sitting.

In my nonchalant scan of the area, I didn't make any eye contact, nor really pay attention to who was sitting there. My mind has been drifting today with thoughts of Dad. Looking to the floor briefly to redirect my thoughts, the shiny black leather shoes catch my attention. Pulling my eyes up the creased silken cloth, the color of black ink; continue trailing up the beautiful paisley tie with colors of black, silver, and gold; resting on the stark white oxford shirt. There's just something about a man in a suit. My eyes finally come to rest on his... *HOLY SHIT!!! Warm and delicious caramel mocha... Master Derek.*

Oh my god, oh my god...what am I going to do? He's beaming that million-dollar smile at me. Does he recognize me? Does he remember that I allowed him to tie me in rope? *He thinks you're crazy as hell 'cause you're standing here just staring at him.*

"Uh...M-Mr. Moore, I'm Debra. Follow me p-please," the words stumbling out of my mouth.

Quickly, I find my place behind my desk and sit before my damn knees buckle under me.

"Have a s-seat." Uh, umm... clearing my throat, I actually try to breathe before continuing. "What can I do for you today?"

"Initially, I came here to get information about a home equity loan. I'm interested in doing some remodeling on my home. Now...I think I'm adding something else to my agenda," he grins with a gleam in his milk chocolate eyes.

"Oh, well I can certainly help you with information about a home equity loan," I offer.

Sinking into the familiarity of work, the nervousness subsides and I provide Derek with all the information he needs and answer all his questions. Gathering all the materials for him and placing them in a folder, I prepare to wrap up our meeting.

"Mr. Moore, is there anything else I can help you with?"

"Please, call me Derek."

I'm blinded by his radiant smile; the smile that causes his eyes to shimmer and my tummy to flip.

"Actually, there is one other thing I want to talk to you about. However, I'm not sure this is the place to discuss it," his radiant smile becoming a little wicked.

"Oh..." I reply perplexed.

"I want to talk to you about *Nexus*," he clarifies.

"*Oh... Nexus,*" I stammer.

"I'm sure you don't want to discuss that here," he chuckles.

"Mmm...no, not really, Mr. Moore. I mean, Derek."

"I don't have to be back to my office until 2pm. Are you free for lunch?"

"Today??? You want to have lunch...today???" I respond dubiously.

"Yes. Unless you have other plans," he retorts with a raised brow.

"No, no plans." I check my watch and it's a little before noon. "I'm free now."

****

We walk just down the sidewalk from the bank to a small bistro. Though it's close in proximity to the bank, I've never eaten here. I fall victim to routine, eating at the same places. Thankfully our table is near the corner with a little more privacy, as I have no idea where this conversation is going to go.

We chit chat a bit about our jobs and I'm surprised to learn he's a prosecutor in the DA's office. *I guess there's all walks of life in the world of kink.* He's so easy to talk to. His voice is smooth as honey and I get lost in his smoldering eyes. I catch myself clenching my sex.

"So, surely you know I remember you from the Open House at Nexus and Katherine's collaring ceremony," he offers.

"I wasn't sure at first...but I definitely remembered you." My sex clenches again as he beams that smile at me, again. *Damn... He's sexy as fuck.*

"I'm not certain of the depth of your relationship with Katherine. Obviously, you are good friends. You came to Open House together and you were at her collaring, as I mentioned earlier. However, I haven't seen you at Nexus since. Why is that?"

"Wow...you cut right to the point," I chuckle. "Katherine and I have been friends for over twen... um, since college. *No need to tell my age.* Going to the Nexus Open House was actually my idea, a girls' night out. Katherine nor I had ever been to a place like Nexus before. We'd only read about them in books. A twist of fate, the stars aligned...Katherine and Isaac connected and fell in love."

"They are great together. I've known Isaac a long time. Katherine has ignited a fire and breathed life back into Isaac's soul. As a longtime friend, it's good to see. But it doesn't answer why you haven't been back?" Derek redirects his question.

"At first, to be honest, a membership to Nexus isn't in my budget. However, after Katherine and Isaac got together, Isaac offered me a membership, as a *Thank you,* for initiating the events that led Katherine to him."

"So what's stopping you? Humor me...there's a reason I'm asking," he grins.

I pause and really ponder his question. I don't know if I feel comfortable sharing my reasons and feelings with him. He's not a stranger, but I don't really know him. Can I trust my feelings with him? *You trusted him at the Open House to completely bind you, leaving you open and vulnerable to him and you'd just laid eyes on him. That was physically vulnerable...this is emotional. I argue with my subconscious.*

"I guess I don't want to feel like a third wheel. I don't really know anyone else there besides Katherine and Isaac, and they'll be together. I would feel very uncomfortable floundering around there on my own," whispering my confession.

"Now you know me, don't you?" His smoldering eyes capture mine, as he leans across the table encompassing my hands with his.

Clenching my sex once again, I feel the dampness between my thighs. A thousand butterflies release in my belly, fluttering all about.

"I-I guess I do," my mouth feeling thick with cotton.

Leaning back, he gives me a respite to gather my thoughts before he proceeds.

"I'm starting a Shibari class at Nexus."

The confused look on my face prompts further explanation from him.

"Shibari is a Japanese Art form of rope bondage. It's what I demonstrated on you at the Open House."

"Oh yes, I remember. I just didn't recall the name," I giddily reply.

"I've been contemplating how I wanted to proceed with the demonstrations for the class. I want it to be authentic. I believe it would be more beneficial for the class to see roadblocks they may encounter during a scene. So the person I'm demonstrating on while I'm teaching, needs to be a novice. Subs I normally demo with are versed and know what my expectations are. To me, that hinders the learning process for the class," he articulates with great emotion. His love of the art form quite evident.

"Makes sense to me. I think it would be very helpful for them."

"I wasn't sure how to make that happen until I saw you today," his smile broadening and eyes gleam.

Perplexity must illuminate my face because he continues his thought process.

"I want you to be my demonstration partner. I think you would be perfect."

"Me???" I gasp.

"Sure, why not? You've had just enough exposure during my demo at Open House to know you don't have any emotional triggers from the bondage; but you're still truly a novice. Plus, it's at Nexus and it will give you a great opportunity to meet more people there. That's why I needed to know the reason you haven't been back. I didn't want to ask, if there was another reason. So what do you say?"

SHIT... what in the hell??? Demonstrating would probably mean no sex. Yet...the one and only time I did this bondage thing, I wanted him to fuck me so bad I couldn't see straight. How in the hell can I demo and not have sex? Go home sexually frustrated...I would need to buy stock in Duracell.

"I-I don't know, Derek," I mumble, while a million thoughts go through my head.

"Oh...In my excitement to ask you, I didn't ask the most important question. Are you married or in a relationship, one that may object to your participation?" His question laced with intrigue.

"Oh no, I'm not married. I've been divorced almost six years and I'm not in a relationship."

"I didn't think so. My assumption based on the fact I don't believe you would have joined me for lunch, otherwise," he surmises.

"True...I wouldn't have."

Leaning across the table once more, he takes my hands in his, piercing me with his gaze while my sex weeps.

"So... what do you say?"

"Y-"

"Fancy seeing you here," the familiar voice interrupting my answer.

The tiny hairs on the back of my neck stand straight up, like a dog with their hackles up in warning. *What the hell is he doing here?* Peering up I make my acknowledgement.

"Hello, Scott. What are you doing here?"

"Aren't you gonna introduce me to your friend, Deb?" Scott's voice feigning interest.

"Scott this is Derek. Derek this is my ex-husband, Scott."

CHAPTER 3

Derek graciously stands and shakes hands with Scott. This is so awkward for me; I can't imagine how Derek is feeling. Though he seems to be taking it all in stride.

"So... what brings you here Scott?" I ask again, trying not to sound rude.

"I had a meeting in town and we decided to have lunch here. I saw you as we got up to leave, so I thought I'd come over and say hi. It's been a while since I've seen you. You're looking good, Deb."

I don't even acknowledge his attempt at a compliment. He keeps standing there like he's expecting me to jump up in his arms or something. *Hell would freeze over first.*

"Well, it was good to see you, Scott. Take care," I announce with as much distance in my words as possible.

After reciprocating my send off, Scott turns and leaves. The only reason he came over was because I'm sitting with a man. If I'd been alone or with another woman, he wouldn't have even considered coming over. Unless he thought he has a chance with the woman. *His lying, cheating, womanizing self...*

"Are you okay, Debra? You seem a little tense," Derek asks calmly.

"I'm fine. He's just trying to nosey in my business. Funny, when we were married, he didn't have time for *my business*. He was too busy being in other women's business," I snicker.

"Seems to me that's his loss," his eyes gleam with a hint of mischief.

"That's sweet of you to say, Derek."

"So, where were we? Ah yes, I remember. I believe you were about to say yes to my request. Am I correct?"

"Yes...I'll give it a try," I respond, drowning in the liquid chocolate of his eyes.

We decide to meet for dinner next week to discuss his ideas for the class in more detail. Derek walks me back to the bank. The short reprieve from the heartbreaking thoughts of Dad was a welcome relief and served to energize me for the remainder of the day.

****

The reprieve is short lived when my phone rings at 3:14am and Mom tells me Dad's fight is over. Deciding to wait until daylight to head back home, I cry myself back to sleep.

Waking shortly after dawn, I contact my boss and implement the vacation I had already arranged and had pending, knowing this day would come sooner rather than later. I'll need to help Mom get things in order and taken care of.

I call Kathy and she insists on driving me down there. I explain I'll be there all week, but she's not taking no for an answer. Isaac's coming to the funeral and she'll ride back with him. She's always been close to my parents, as hers passed away a long time ago. Kathy's sons, Matt and Ben, are my Godsons and my parents are the only grandparents they've ever known. And being I have no children, my parents treated those boys like their own grandchildren. It was a perfect match.

****

The service was beautiful. I'm so thankful Kathy's been here the past couple of days. She's been a tremendous help with Mom, well...until Isaac arrived. He came down yesterday and Mom has consumed every minute of his waking hour. He's doting over her and she's eating it up. He's been so sweet with her.

I can't believe Matt and Ben took time away from their busy college schedule and drove here for the funeral, too. The boys helped Isaac with some handy work around the house that's been neglected since Dad got sick. Isaac also offered to send a crew down to finish the sunroom Dad started two years ago, before he got so sick. He's such a good man. I'm so happy Kathy found him. She had such a hard life raising those boys on her own.

Mom broke down crying, hell, we all did, as Matt and Ben gave the eulogy as proud "grandsons". Even Scott was a little teary eyed, when I glanced over at him.

It was thoughtful of Scott to come today and pay his respects. My parents loved him. They were aware of the one incident of Scott's infidelity, but I was too ashamed to share with them all of the times that I was blind to his indiscretions. When we first separated, they encouraged me to give him another chance.

I think Scott regrets not having children, though he always acted like he was fine not having them. We tried when we were first married. The doctors said sometimes when you've been on birth control for a long time, it takes a while for your system to regulate. We didn't use birth control for three years. I got pregnant once, miscarrying by the ninth week. We had tests done, but nothing conclusive that prevented pregnancy. We couldn't afford In Vitro and I honestly didn't know if I wanted to go that route. I figured if it was meant to be, I would get pregnant naturally. As it turned out, it was the best thing. Scott had multiple affairs throughout our marriage, unbeknownst to me, until the last one and our marriage ended. I'm thankful every day that I didn't have to drag children through that mess.

"If you're sure you're okay, we're gonna head home," Kathy says hugging my neck, bringing my thoughts back to the present.

"Yes...I'm good. Thank you so much for being here with me the past few days. I don't know if I could've handled Mom alone."

"I wouldn't have been anywhere else, but by your side sweetie. You know I love you," she exhales as I embrace her.

Releasing Kathy, I wrap my arms around Isaac and he engulfs me in his.

"Thank you, Isaac, for everything you and the boys did around the house and for being so sweet with Mom. I think she would like to keep you," I chuckle.

"Glad I could help out some. I'll have a crew come down in a few weeks to finish the room. We should be able to do it in a day," Isaac replies, releasing his hug.

"And thanks for letting me steal Kathy for a few days. I don't know what I would've done without her," my voice begins to crack, tears welling in my eyes.

"I knew it was a package deal with Peaches; her, the boys, and you," Isaac chuckles. "I know her and this is where she needed to be."

****

All the voices that filled the house are gone. Mom decided to go to my aunt's house for the night. I think it's a good idea for her to get out of the house. I suddenly feel exhausted, so I curl up on the sofa, leaning back on the pillows, supporting my heavy head. The silence allows my mind to wonder. I tried to be strong for Mom, keeping my emotions to myself. Thoughts of Dad and my life, I close my eyes and the tears begin to flow.

I don't know how much time passes before the stroke of a finger down my cheek, lulls me into a lethargic state.

"It's okay babe, I'm here," the all too familiar voice, soothing my grief.

My eyes remain closed, allowing my body to succumb to the comfort. I feel his breath upon my face and sense his energy surrounding my body. His lips touch mine, the taste of salt from my tears mingle with his minty breath. His tongue caresses my lips, requesting entry. My mouth relaxes under his tongue's insistence and he makes haste delving between my lips. Our mouths tangle with ebb and flow. I have no thoughts in my head, only intent on losing myself in comfort and forgetting the pain.

His hands begin an exploration of their own. Skillfully manipulating the buttons on my blouse until it falls open and cool air electrifies the dampness forming on my chest. As if no impediment whatsoever, the front clasp is unhinged and the band on my bra contracts, exposing the rose red pebbles.

He abruptly breaks the tango of our tongues, immediately using his to swirl around my hardened nub, sucking it between his lips. I let out a groan and I feel his cock grinding into my belly. My thoughts are all over the place. Dreaming...

I feel his hand fumbling with my skirt, maneuvering it up to my thighs. His hand retreats back between my legs, stroking the tender flesh between, as it travels toward my sex. His fingers push my panties to the side, slipping past the material, sinking deep in my sex.

"You're so wet...I'm gonna sink deep in your cunt."

My eyes fly wide open and my heart begins pounding in my chest. *What the fuck?!?!?!*

"Stop!" I cry out.

"It's okay, I got a condom, babe."

"No, stop! I can't do this. This is a mistake." I urge, pushing my hands to his chest.

"My cock is throbbing Deb. I'm about to explode," he grouses, putting the head of his cock at my entrance.

"NO SCOTT...STOP!!!" I yell, pushing him away.

"What the fuck???" He growls back at me.

"This is wrong. I wasn't thinking." *Not about you, anyways.* "You're taking advantage of an emotional situation."

"You didn't stop me...not at first."

"I was crying. I'm hurt. My dad died. I'm a little emotional. Give me a break... What are you doing here anyways? I thought everyone was gone."

"I took a walk. When I got back, I came in through the kitchen door. I saw you lying here and... Well, I couldn't resist."

"Yeah, I recall from our marriage, you having difficulty *resisting* women," I snarl.

Straightening my clothes and gathering my wits, I go to the kitchen in search of comfort...from food.

What in the hell??? One moment of weakness and fucking Scott pounces. I knew subconsciously it was him, but I was drowning in sorrow and just needed comforting. I lost connection that it was him, my thoughts were all over the place. A face I couldn't make out in my head.... It was faceless, so I just let go. How stupid!!! Thankfully, it didn't go any farther.

I'm savoring each bite of Cheesecake, when Scott saunters over beside me.

"So... what are you doing, Deb?"

Umm, eating Cheesecake, dumbass. "What are you referring to, Scott?"

"The guy at the restaurant the other day."

"Not that it's any of your business, but it was *business*."

"Bullshit! I saw him holding your hands, that's not business. You're making a fool of yourself being seen out with that guy."

"EXCUSE ME!!!"

"You heard me and you know I'm right. You're embarrassing yourself, as well as me."

"WHAT!?!?!" I scream, shaking my head to make sense of what he's saying.

"You know what I'm talking about, Deb?"

"No...I don't know. Enlighten me," I sneer.

"He's too young for you, Deb. Are you one of those *cougars?*"

"COUGAR!!! Are you kidding me??? You fucking chauvinist pig!!! How many tramps did you screw around with that were younger than you? Huh...yeah that's right, ALL OF THEM!!!"

Aaarrgg...the nerve of this man. I want to knock the shit out of him. He's telling me I'm *too old* for Derek, but he can fuck around with any twenty something twat that he wants to. Besides...Derek's not that much younger. *Who cares if he is? And, it is business. What am I doing? I don't owe him an explanation. Fuck him!!!*

"Look...I think it's time for you to go. It's been a long day for me."

"I understand and I'll go, but there's something I've been needing to tell you."

"Go on."

"I'm getting married again."

"Whoa...wait a minute! You just had your tongue down my throat, sucking on my tits, your fingers deep in my pussy; wanting to sink your cock in. And you tell me now, you're getting married..." Shaking my head, "I don't know her, but I feel sorry for her. I hope she finds out what a piece of shit you are before it's too late. GET the fuck OUT!!!"

CHAPTER 4

Getting back to work and back into life's routine has been really beneficial for me. I hated leaving Mom alone, but she has a great group of friends in her social circle and they will keep her busy. I'm looking forward to lunch with Kathy today. We have a lot to talk about.

The morning has flown by, as I try to make a dent in the work that piled up while I was away. Responding to emails alone, took up a large chunk of the morning. Deep in thought, I startle when I look up and see a woman standing at my door holding the most beautiful flowers I've ever seen.

"Debra Jenkins...," whispers the lady standing at my door.

"Yes..." I reply, making my way over to her.

"I have a delivery for you," she responds, extending me the flower vase she's holding in her hands.

Thanking her, I return to my chair, placing the flowers in the middle of my desk, to admire. Gorgeous, long stemmed, white Calla

Lilies with a beautiful black lace bow surrounding the vase. Having no clue who would send me flowers, I excidedly open the card.

My Deepest Sympathy for
The loss of your Father.
I look forward to our dinner on Thursday.

Derek

Oh my gosh...I can't believe Derek sent me flowers. So sweet and thoughtful. They are stunning. I can't help staring at them. I grab my phone and take a picture to send to Kathy.

ME: Look what I just got!!! Guess who sent them???
KATHY: OMG...They're BEAUTIFUL!!!   From who???
ME: I'll share that at lunch... LOL!
KATHY: Tease...

I scroll through my phone to find Derek's number and make a quick call to thank him for the flowers. The call goes to his voicemail and I leave him a message. I'll follow up later this afternoon. Refocusing on my work, I repeatedly look up to glance at the stunning arrangement; butterflies taking flight in my belly each time.

****

"So who are the flowers from?" Kathy demands before I even have a chance to sit down.

"Well, hello to you to," I reply, feigning hurt feelings.

"Oh, hey...now, who sent the flowers?"

"Well..." I leave the word lingering in the air.

"That's a deep subject. I just want to know who sent the flowers," Kathy smirks with dry humor.

"Okay, okay... The flowers are from Derek. Can you believe it?"

"No way...really??? Is there something you're not telling me?" Kathy asks skeptically.

"What? No... I told you about him coming to the bank, going to lunch, and him asking me to partner with him for demonstrations for his rope classes. Shitari, Shabuki, or something like that. I can't remember the name right now. Anyways, we agreed to meet for dinner on Thursday for him to go over more details. The card with the flowers offered his condolences and said he was looking forward to our dinner," I explain. "It's so thoughtful of him."

"That is very sweet of him. He's truly a kind and considerate person; always thinking of others. He's so soft spoken, it was hard at first for me to imagine him as a Master. However, I've witnessed his scenes first hand and he has a very commanding presence about him. I really like Derek.

I'm just so excited that you're actually coming to Nexus. You wouldn't come when *I* asked you, but let a smokin' hot Dom ask you and you relent," Kathy gleans.

"Yeah...well, when your ass looks like his, you might have a little more persuasion with me."

Our conversation continues, expanding to my dress attire for Thursday night's dinner onto most importantly what to wear to Nexus. Kathy makes a great point, that maybe I should talk with Derek about that, being that I'm gonna be literally tied up in knots and some things may be more appropriate than others.

My world can be upside down and a complete mess, but then I talk things through with Kathy and she makes the world seem right again.

"So, I have a bit of news to share," announces Kathy, raising her eyebrow.

"Oh shit...You're pregnant!"

"WHAT!?!?! Uh, *NO*... Are you insane??? You know that can't happen. I took care of that when Matt was born."

"Hey...crazier things have happened. I've heard of women's tubes growing back together and they get pregnant; usually in their 40's."

"Shut your mouth! Don't you speak it to existence" Kathy grouses at me.

"What? Isaac may want a baby," I continue agitating her.

"Shut the hell up. He doesn't and I'm too old to start again. Besides, I have a lot of sex to catch up on. It took me over 40 years to find out what it means to be thoroughly fucked."

I roar with laughter and now we're both cackling like hens. People are beginning to stare, but I could care less. With intermittent shudders of giggles, our laughter is under control within a few minutes.

"Uh, hmmm...so what's your news?" I ask, still trying to calm my giggles.

"I've told you about Ms. Glancey, Isaac's secretary," Kathy states, wiping the last tears of laughter from her eyes. "She had a heart attack almost a year ago and Isaac tried to get her to retire. She refused, saying Isaac needed her and he admits that he did. She's been with the company for a very long time. She was Isaac's father's secretary when he ran the company. Anyway...she's finally decided to retire."

"Really? Well, good for her. What changed her mind?"

"I'm not exactly sure. She's in her seventies and Isaac has been encouraging her for a while. But...that's not the news. The *news* is... Isaac wants me to come to work for him."

"Don't you already work for him?"

"Yeah, at Nexus. Now he wants me to work for him at J & J Contractors. Basically taking over for Ms. Glancey, as well as taking over the accounting."

"Wow...what are you gonna do? You've been at your current job a long time."

"Yeah, I've been with Atlanta Media for over 14 years. I don't know what to do. We live together, about to be married and we work part-time together at Nexus. Though he really doesn't have much to do with the business aspect of it anymore. I'm just afraid with all of that and add working *every* day together, may be too much. I can see my ass getting blistered every day, and not necessarily in a good way. And... he may get tired of me."

"Tired of you??? Girl that man worships the ground you walk on. You can make excuses if you want, but that's not one of them," I chide.

I can't help but laugh, even though I can't imagine making that kind of decision. I understand her apprehensiveness. That's a lot of time together. I don't care how much you love someone, you need some time to yourself, every once in a while.

"I think my upcoming business trip to Chicago has something to do with his urgency for this job change. It's my first trip since the incident in Memphis and Isaac doesn't want me to go. I'm a little nervous about going, but I have to face my fear or cower the rest of my life. Isaac is a protector and he likes to be in control. He's limited in those capacities with me working for Atlanta Media and having to travel. The Chicago trip has put it in the forefront of his mind."

"Well, to be honest Kathy, I don't want you traveling by yourself, either. When Isaac called and told me what happened in Memphis, I got physically sick. Especially, that it was someone you knew," I shiver recalling seeing her bruised and swollen face and busted lip for the first time.

Kathy reaches over and squeezes my hand, "I know. I don't even like to think about what would've happened if Isaac hadn't shown up when he did."

"What's going on with the case?" I ask.

"Rick is still in jail for the time being. If he makes bail, he can get out. I have a restraining order in place in the event he makes bail before court, which is likely since it will probably be next year before we go. However, they're really not worth the paper they're written on if the person chooses not to abide by it. Patrick is still investigating links between Rick and other unsolved sexual assault cases, but I don't know if he has any leads," Kathy continues.

"So, Patrick is still working your case?" I ask, just a little too eager.

"Yeah... When the assault in Memphis occurred and the realization that it was Rick who broke in my house, Patrick continued working the case here, hoping to solve the other cases. The DA is working to have both of my cases consolidated into one indictment here, so we don't have to travel to Memphis for a trial."

"Hmmm..." *I can think of some investigating Patrick can do.* "One trial would make it a lot easier on you."

"Hmmm, yourself...I know that look, chick. Your face lights up at the mention of Patrick's name," Kathy teases.

"You're crazy..."

"Umm, *okay*...whatever you say, Deb." Looking at her watch, Kathy continues, "I need to get back to work. Thanks for letting me vent about Isaac's job proposal. It always helps me to see things clearer when I vocalize them."

"Always...you know that. You've helped me through more than I care to remember. Helping out with Mom last week, has me indebted to you for life," I snicker. "Hell, I owe Isaac my right arm.

He charmed the hell out of Mom. She gushed about him all weekend."

We end our lunch with another tear filled laugh.

****

It should be a sin to look as good as this man does. A mint green dress shirt, perfectly tailored to accent his muscular torso; untucked and unbuttoned at the top, offering a peak of deliciousness. Dark denim snugs his round ass; a perfect handful in each hand. All this and he's sitting across from me.

I'm sure he's been explaining something I need to know about his rope class, but for the life of me I can't pay attention. I'm mesmerized, not only by his looks, but his voice drips honey when he speaks. I'm stuck in an 'awe-like' state. His passion for his lifestyle is evident in every word he speaks.

"So, Derek...how long have you been living this lifestyle, in the lifestyle? I'm really not sure how to refer to it," I admit.

"That's the great thing about *this lifestyle*; there's no right way or wrong way to do anything. It's your way. The way you and your partner agree and choose to live it. I call it living *my life*. If anybody tells you differently...they're wrong, don't listen to them.

Back to your question...I've been living *my life* over 12 years. I dabbled in the scene in college and law school, but I didn't get serious in learning about it until I met Isaac. I hadn't been out of law school long, just started practicing law when I was hired by Isaac to handle his divorce. In discussing matters of his divorce, the BDSM lifestyle came up. I was intrigued, but held off discussing it with him until my professional obligation to him was over."

"So you've known Isaac since before he opened Nexus?" I ask, struggling to keep the shock out of my voice.

Laughing, Derek replies, "I am member number one. Isaac bought the plantation home at an auction about 6 months after his divorce was final. He took me under his wing and taught me most everything I know about the lifestyle. When I took a liking to Shibari, he referred me to the man who had guided him."

All of this insight into Derek and *Isaac*, has left me speechless, something that rarely happens. I'm trying to digest all this information. I had no idea their connection is so strong, spanning over 10 years.

"Huh...I had no idea you've known Isaac so long."

"I may have a few more surprises for you. You, just never know," Derek entices with a wicked grin.

My belly flips and I clench my sex so tight, I think I'll come if one breath from his mouth lands on me.

Attuned to my lack of ability to communicate, Derek directs the conversation, "I think it would be a good idea for us to familiarize ourselves with each other and you with Nexus, before the class starts."

Familiarize ourselves with each other.......Holy shit.

Derek continues, "If you're free Saturday night, I would like you to accompany me to Nexus."

CHAPTER 5

Thankfully, with a tug here and there, this little yellow dress still fits. I think I gained ten pounds staying at my parents for a week. I couldn't resist all the scrumptious food that friends and family shared with us.

I can't believe I've agreed to all this; being put on display for Derek's class and now going to Nexus with him to 'familiarize ourselves with each other'. *I could have gotten familiar with him the other night after dinner. But no... He's too much of a freakin' gentleman. Not even a kiss, well, the peck on the cheek don't count. However, his lips seared my skin.*

A quick knock on the door halts my reminiscent thoughts. Feeling like a penguin walking in this tight dress, my baby steps finally bring me to the foyer. Opening the door, an eye-fucking commences.

Holy hell...black silk shirt, closed with a few buttons from the chest down. Black leather pants that cling to every ridge of muscle in his thighs. I drink in every drop of his essence like a desert nomad dying of thirst. A black shadow neatly outlines his angular jaw, mimicking the shadow of hair atop his head; all accenting his delicious caramelized skin. The smoldering look in his eyes and wicked smile offer a dark, mysterious side to Derek that I've never seen. Tall, Dark, and sexy as fuck...

"WOW... Hello Sunshine! You look amazing!" Derek exclaims with his killer smile.

"Ummm, you look pretty amazing yourself, Sir." *Sir??? Well that just tumbled out.*

"I like the way that rolls off your lips, Sunshine," his voice dropping an octave.

"Um...I'm sorry. What???"

"*Sir*...I like the way *Sir* rolls off your lips."

And the weeping of my sex begins, with no doubt it becoming a waterfall by nights' end.

****

The synthesizing rhythm is flowing from beyond the walls of the lobby. Thankful for Derek's pep talk on the drive over, explaining the basic *dos and don'ts*, which is basically using good manners for the most part. My tummy is flipping like a fish out of water. Maybe I should heed the warning, as I am clearly out of my element and I'm only in the lobby. When I came for Open House, it was different. I knew there were others here like myself, just wanting a peek inside the life. Tonight, it's the real deal. I'm not just sneaking a peek, I'm part of this life, now. *Oh my god...what am I doing???*

The blond bombshell I remember from the Open House, greets us as we approach the sign in desk.

"Good evening Master Derek. Who do we have with us tonight?" Blondie's bubbly voice borders irritation at the onset.

"Good evening Gina, this is Debra Jenkins. She'll be assisting me with Shibari classes on Thursday nights, starting next week. She should be on the member list. I turned in her medical forms to Isaac last night," Derek advises.

"It's nice to meet you, Gina," I nod and smile to the giddy beauty.

"Welcome Debra! You're a friend of Kathy's, aren't you?"

"Yes, I am."

"Yay! I remember her mentioning you before. Kathy and Isaac are out in the club. You'll probably see them out there. Welcome again! I'm sure you'll love it here."

"Thanks! I'm sure I will."

Derek gently places his hand at the small of my back leading me around the wall separating the lobby from the rest of the club. The music lulls me into its erotic rhythm and immediately begins seducing my mind. I've always loved 'Closer' by the Kings of Leon, but hearing it in this setting; bodies grinding on the dance floor with no inhibitions, has a very sexual effect on me. Not that I need any more stimulation in that area. My body zings with every touch of Derek's hand.

I'm trying to absorb all the sights and sounds and keep my mouth from gaping wide. I'm not very good at multi-tasking. Derek's hand remains just above my ass, while I pan the room slowly from side to side. He applies slight pressure to my back, guiding me toward the bar.

Holy Hotness... A tall guy, *hell they're all tall compared to my short stature*, with short, dirty blonde hair, mussed about right in front, is standing behind the bar. His chest is perfectly bare, without a single blemish or mark. I could so lean over and run my tongue around his firm nips.

"Hey Zeke, this is Debra," Derek introduces. "She'll be assisting me with the Shibari classes."

We exchange introductions and I try to steady my knees to keep from falling on my face. Derek and Zeke chit chat a bit while I continue perusing the happenings going on around me. So far, it's been pretty calm, nothing too outrageous. The music has drowned out most of the sounds that I remember hearing before when I was here. However, the distinct smell of rich leather entwined with lust and sex can't be diminished.

"Are you ready to explore?" Derek asks suggestively.

"Yes, Sir."

Derek begins my tour of Nexus and we casually walk from station to station.

"Is Zeke a Master?"

"No...not yet. He's in the beginning stages of training with Isaac to become a Master. The only Masters at Nexus are Isaac, Patrick, and myself."

"What does it mean to be a *Master*?"

"It means different things at different places. Here at Nexus, it means you've been trained in the varying techniques of play allowed, as well as safety and psychological protocol for Doms and subs, alike."

"I know you were trained by Master Isaac, but what about Master Patrick?" My inquisition continuing.

"Patrick and I have been friends since high school. He dabbled in the scene during college, like I did, but didn't get serious with it. After Nexus opened, he saw how the lifestyle could be for him through the right training, so he joined and like me, Isaac took him under his wing."

Damn, this man has to stop dropping these bombs of information on me. *Derek and Patrick have been friends since high school???* We stop behind a small gathering of people watching a scene. I immediately recognize the stunning, petite blond with the strong resemblance to Gwen Stefani, from Open House. *Mistress Charlotte...*

A moment passes and I'm utterly confused. Mistress Charlotte is sitting off to the side, while her sub Edward, is flailing a flogger across the back of a tall, statuesque brunette. The buxom brunette's head dangles forward. *This is not the Edward I saw at Open House, crawling on all fours, led around with a leash, kissing Mistress Charlotte's boots, with his cock in a cage.*

Edward unshackles the brunette, fists his hand in her hair and guides her over to Mistress Charlotte in the chair. Edward nudges the woman to her knees and guides her between Mistress Charlotte's legs. Mistress opens her legs, showcasing her bare mound. The woman leans forward and her tongue delves between the moistened lips of Charlotte's sex. Simultaneously, Edward has fitted his cock with a condom, dropped to his knees and sunk balls deep into the brunette's drenched sex, causing her to release a moan in Charlotte's. Edward strokes slowly to avoid disrupting the brunette from devouring Charlotte.

Moments later, Charlotte maneuvers the brunette away. Edward continues his slow thrusts into the brunette. Charlotte appears to be putting on some type of harness, but I can't really tell what she's doing. She taps Edward's shoulder and he immediately withdraws his cock and removes the condom. He repositions the brunette, placing her face at his crotch and thrusting his cock between her lips; the woman at his mercy, or lack thereof.

My sex is throbbing and I'm squeezing my thighs together to halt the sensation. Like a train wreck, I can't tear my eyes away. This is no blowjob, Edward is literally fucking her face. I think I've seen it all and can take no more without a nuclear meltdown, when Charlotte turns and drops to her knees, thrusting a huge dildo deep into the brunette's sex. An animalistic sound roars from the lips around Edward's cock; the brunette, trapped between the Domme and *Dom??? Holy shit... they've completely reversed.*

Charlotte thrusts slow and sensual, in and out of the brunette's sex..., in and out. Edward continues pumping his cock between the swollen lips of the buxom beauty, until he roars; ropes of his release coating the brunettes back. Charlotte increases her thrusts, while reaching around stroking the woman's clit.

Edward appears to be attending to hygiene over in the corner while Charlotte continues sensually thrusting the thick phallus deep in the brunette's sex. There's a continual moan coming from the sated woman, as her eyes glaze over.

Edward comes over to stand beside the women entangled on the floor, stroking himself as he watches the erotic scene. I am beside myself as I witness his cock firm. Edward fits on another condom and kneels behind Charlotte. Flipping her skirt upon her back, Edward spreads Charlotte's ass cheeks and slowly sinks his cock between her glistening folds. Her head drops forward as a faint groan escapes her.

Awkward at first, the trio quickly synchronize their movement. Edward hovers over Charlotte's tiny physique as he thrusts into her, controlling her thrust into the brunette; who's in a submissive presentation. Charlotte has one hand on the Brunette's back, while fondling the woman's right breast. Edward begins to stroke Charlotte's clit and she in return mimics this with the brunette. Both women are clearly on the verge of an orgasmic explosion.

This is the most unimaginable, most erotic thing I've ever witnessed. Clearly evident by my own essence drizzling down my thigh.

Edward begins pounding into Charlotte, and she into the brunette. Charlotte reaches around again gripping the brunette's clit, pinching until the woman screams her release and collapses to the floor. Edward pumps furiously into Charlotte. Their roles blurring, making it difficult to distinguish the dominant in this relationship. Edward towers over Charlotte's submissive form, drilling her mercilessly. Charlotte's slacken body has relented and what I can only describe as ecstasy, shows in her eyes. Gripping a hardened tip with one hand and her clit with the other, Edward pulls on both, sending an inhumane cry ripping from Charlotte, as he roars his release.

I shiver my own mini release as Derek wraps his arms around mine and places a kiss softly on my neck. I melt into his chest in utter amazement at the display of eroticism. *What in the world did I just witness??? Edward's behavior was not that of any sub I've ever read about. If he's not a dominant, then I don't know who is.*

"Ummm...what just happened here? I'm so confused," I whisper in the air.

"I wanted to ease you gently into your surroundings here, just get your toes wet. However, you got knocked in the deep end. When I realized what was going to take place in that scene, you were already completely enthralled in it. Your pulse increased and your breathing shallowed..." Leaning down, Derek whispers in my ear, "By your shudder, I believe you enjoyed it. Yes???"

Heat from embarrassment creeps from my chest to my face, as moisture continues to seep between my thighs. *What have I gotten myself into??? I'm going to make a fool of myself here, leaving puddles at every scene I stop at. I'm like Hansel and Gretel, only I can follow the drizzling from my sex to find my way out of this erotic haven.*

We've barely made it in the door and I already feel like a sex-depraved nymphomaniac needing my next fix. I need to be fucked and fucked NOW!!!

CHAPTER 6

Derek and I continue our journey from scene to scene. We pass one area and while I'm trying to discern the wooden, guillotine-looking contraption, I notice Isaac sitting in an oversized, plush arm chair with his arms wrapped around Kathy, cuddling her in his lap.

"What is that?" I ask Derek, pointing to the piece of wooden equipment.

"It's called a stockade; it's used for bondage."

A mini movie begins playing in my mind, imagining the scene that has apparently just played out between Kathy and Isaac.

"Isaac is performing aftercare with Katherine; the most critical element of a scene," Derek explains, my curiosity obviously showing on my face. "Aftercare includes hugging, kissing, stroking, cuddling, words of praise; forming an emotional bond between partners."

Allowing his teaching moment to sink in, Derek and I proceed on, without disturbing the couple snuggling in the corner.

My mind can't process my surroundings fast enough. Lust, leather, and sex permeate through my senses. Every ounce of my being is charged and electrified. We approach another scene, stopping just behind the small gathering of people. There's a man and woman in the scene with their backs to us. Without seeing his face, I immediately recognize the man by the tattooed wing expanding over his right shoulder. *Master Patrick...*

The young woman is bound to a wooden cross by her wrists and ankles, as Patrick lands lash after lash of the flogger, across her back; the thud rumbling through the air. A burning twinge streaks through my chest. Envy or *jealousy*??? *It can't be jealousy...Patrick doesn't belong to me.* Whatever it is...I don't like the feeling.

"Isn't that Pa- umm, I mean Master Patrick? I think I remember him from Open House." I ask, clearly unable to control my nosiness.

"Yes, that's Master Patrick training with Alexandria. She's a new sub. Master Patrick and I are responsible for training new subs at Nexus. Isaac used to, but he resigned from training when he collared Katherine."

Training, huh...

"Training subs? What does that mean?" I continue my inquiry.

"Submissives interested in learning about the lifestyle, but don't have a partner or dominant, can receive training to prepare them for when they do meet a potential partner."

"Hmmm...," my reeling mind unable to form a sentence.

"Is that something you'd be interested in, Debra?"

Derek's question catches me completely off guard. "Uh...well, I really haven't given any thought to it." Which is the truth because I didn't know such a thing existed. *Training for submissives...*

"Well, it's definitely an option available to you. I highly recommend it, if you're interested in delving deeper in the lifestyle."

"Thank you, Master Derek. I will definitely keep it in mind."

But the only thing I can focus on right now is the sheen of perspiration forming across Patrick's well-defined, muscular shoulders; pooling in the hollow of his back, streaming toward his round ass. *Oh to be a droplet of sweat right now...*

Patrick's hands now caress the body of the woman at his mercy, speaking softly into her ear. The unnerving twinge pricks at my heart again. Their connection appears very intimate at first glance. My initial impression of the duo's relationship is that it's of a sexual nature; with the tender caresses. Yet, as I continue observing their interaction, I realize it's not sexual at all. This confounds me because my own sex is damp and throbbing with need.

Master Patrick is definitely caring for the woman, stroking his finger down her cheek, massaging her neck and shoulders.

However, there's no fondling or kissing or petting. Though I have no doubt, the woman, *Alexandria... I think is her name*, is starving for something more.

"Do these scenes usually end with...um...*sex*? I whisper in embarrassment.

"Actually, most scenes don't. There are many emotional and physical needs, in varying degrees, met among the participants in a scene. Sex is a derivative of those needs being met. Sex is a physical release, an emotional connection, or both. Sometimes a person needs that and sometimes they don't."

"You're very insightful, Master Derek. Thought provoking..."

"I don't know how insightful I am; just lessons I've learned. The exception to that is training. When training a sub, there are goals to meet. The feeling is typically clinical. However, if there's a strong attraction, as such with Isaac and Katherine, the dynamic of the relationship changes from teacher/pupil to something more intimate."

Damn, I can't resist the urge to stick my nose where it doesn't belong. *Don't ask it, do...not...ask...it. Shit...shit...shit. I'm asking...*

"So...is Patrick and um, Ale..."

"Alexandria?"

"Yes...Alexandria. Are they a couple? Patrick and Alexandria?" My words stumbling out of my mouth.

"Not to my knowledge. Why? Do you have an interest?"

"Who? Me? Oh, no... No, not me. I'm just curious." *Holy shit...Derek just called me out. I need to shut the hell up. I'm babbling on like the town idiot, making a fool of myself.*

Responding with only a wicked grin, Derek takes my hand and leads me away. We walk a short distance down a hall and stop in front of an unoccupied area. It's cordoned off, somewhat private, but no door.

There's an oversized chair off to the side, identical to the chair Isaac was sitting in with Kathy. A small chest with drawers is near the comfy looking chair. I notice a leather duffle bag on top of the chest. Panning the area, my eyes land on an awkward looking chair near the back of the area. It looks similar to a weight bench in a gym, but one that's been split in half and folded in on itself.

"I think we need to get to know each other a little better," Derek whispers in my ear.

The vibration of his voice resonates a warm sensation throughout my body, igniting a fire in my core. The waning quiver in my sex regains momentum, building to a delicious pulsating rhythm. I squeeze my thighs together in an effort to thwart the sinful rhythm from taking over my body.

Derek guides me over to the medieval looking chair, manipulating my body upon the odd contraption. My thighs are supported on separate padded platforms, spreading them wide. This causes my dress to ride up, almost completely exposing my ass. My legs are supported, but my ass is suspended between the platforms, allowing complete access to my ass and drenched sex.

Derek kneels down and I feel a soft cuff surround my ankle. Instinctively I try to move my leg, but to no avail. The cuff is soft against my skin, but firm in its hold. He repeats the procedure on my other ankle. Within a couple minutes, Derek has my wrists bound to smaller, padded platforms on each side of my head; both arms raised, mimicking the universal sign of surrender. Which is exactly what I've done; without a single word communicated between us. Apprehension and excitement intermingle, sending currents of electricity pinging throughout my body. As if my body weren't electrified enough, a bolt of lightning strikes down my spine when Derek places a blindfold over my eyes and I'm thrust into darkness.

My abdication has given all control to Derek with no resistance. I'm completely and utterly, at his mercy. His finger is stroking my sensitive inner thigh.

"Debra, your safeword is red."

"Yes, Sir," I reply breathlessly.

The soft stroking on the inside of my thigh continues, moving closer to my sex. Oh my god, I feel his warm breath on my mons. Impulsively, I try to squeeze my legs together. *Ummm...that's not gonna work.*

"Though I normally like a bare pussy, your small, designer groomed triangle is sexy."

Shit... I know he can see how wet I am.

"It's supposed to be a martini design," I blurt out, like he really cares.

"Yes...I can see that now," his finger tracing the outline of the design.

His breath feels so warm on my sodden folds. Unconsciously, my hips move toward the warmth. I'm aching to feel his mouth on me. Literally trembling with need. A swat to my outer thigh halts the growing need.

"Tsk, Tsk, Sunshine. I believe I have a wanton wench on my hands. Unfortunately for you, I'm in control here, not you."

A whispering growl escapes my lips and another smack lands on my thigh. The sting of his hand morphs into fuel for the fire in my core.

"Would you like to come, Sunshine?"

"Y-yes. Yes, Sir. Please...," I whisper.

"Then I suggest not growling at me. Moaning...yes. Growling... That gets your orgasm denied."

His wicked chuckle spawns another growl from me and that spawns another whack to my thigh. *Sting...fuel...fire. Sting...fuel...fire. STING, FUEL, FIRE! A vicious circle and battle of wills that I'm losing. Derek Moore will be my demise.*

A tug at the top of my dress and it loosens slightly as I hear the teeth of the zipper unhinge, making the familiar zipping sound. It stops midway down my abdomen. My nubs constrict and harden further when the cool air drifts across the tips.

Something prickles the sensitive skin of my areola; strategically circling the pebbled tip. I'm torn with wanting the prickling sensation to graze over the ultra-sensitive nip and avoiding it all together.

Proving there's no need for me to even ponder such thoughts, Derek transverses the prickling device across the hardened nip, sending an electrical charge straight to my clit. Derek continues his perusing with his needle-like device, over both of my breasts.

The sensation suddenly begins to travel down my abdomen, across my mons, and directly over my pulsating clit, without hesitation. The movement so quick and my mind drowning in arousal, I barely have time to register what was happening before the sensation sets off an explosion in my core.

"OH MY GOD!!!" My heart is pounding and I feel beads of sweat forming on my brow. Tremors have overtaken my body. He's barely touched me and I feel like I'm about to combust. I'm so freakin' pathetic...

Warm, wetness flicks over my constricted nub, before his lips clasp around my tiny breast, literally sucking it entirely in his mouth. Sucking and then flicking the tip with his tongue sends me into a writhing fit.

I feel his finger caressing between my sodden folds and he pauses at the opening of my sex. My mind is willing him to penetrate, but he lingers there while he devours my right breast.

"You're so wet, Sunshine." I hear a sucking, smacking sound. "And you taste so sweet."

Holy shit...he must've licked his finger.

He begins to ravish my left breast again, as he sinks a finger deep in my sex. A long and low moan escapes me.

"That's what I want to hear, Sunshine," he groans in my ear while he begins to move his long finger in and out of my sex. "But don't come until I say. You want to please me, don't you?"

"Yes, Sir. But I don't think..." His finger lightly covers my mouth.

"Sshhh... It's not your job to think, Debra. You want to please me and you will."

"Yes, Sir."

"That's a Good Girl."

His rhythm increases and he adds what feels like another finger into my sex, while another begins to massage my clit. I begin grinding my hips into each of his thrusts. *Oh my god...it feels so fuckin' good.* Pressure is building in my core. I don't know how much more I can take.

"You're so wet. Do you like grinding your pussy on my hand, baby?"

"Yes...Sir," I pant.

"I want to look into your eyes when you come." With that said, light penetrates my eyes as the blindfold comes off. I squint trying to adjust to the sudden brightness.

Derek never skips a beat and my mind drifts away again under the onslaught of his finger fucking.

"Eyes on me, Sunshine. Eyes on me."

I struggle to keep my eyes from rolling back in my head and focus on him. He breaks his gaze, assaulting my breast again. He grips my hardened nub between his teeth, sending a shockwave straight to my clit.

"Oh god, Sir. I'm gonna come...I need to come," I cry out.

"Not til I say, Sunshine. I know you want to please me and waiting for my permission will please me."

God...how does he have this much control. Do I have no effect on him? Does THIS have no effect?

I shift my eyes downward. Considering the enormous bulge straining his leather pants, I would say he's definitely not immune. *He just obviously has better self-control.*

"Eyes Debra...," he demands, his voice lowering an octave. *Oh shit...*

He pumps his fingers a few more times, curving inward. I've never felt these sensations before. My legs are quivering, from just a finger fucking.

"I want you to drench my hand. Come for me, baby...come now," he growls, as he thrusts hard and pinches my clit. An indecipherable sound erupts from my chest and I shatter beneath his hand.

CHAPTER 7

My panting finally slows to shallow breathing. To my surprise, I'm snuggled up to a bare chest and my hair is being stroked. Stirring a bit and re-focusing, I sit up slightly and realize I'm sitting on Derek's lap in the chair in the corner. *Damn, I must have been out of it.*

"There she is. How do you feel?" Derek's soft voice whispers in my ear.

"I'm good, but did I pass out? I don't remember coming over to the chair."

"I think you reached a level of subspace."

"Excuse me...what?" Sitting up straighter.

"Subspace is a euphoric, trance-like state brought on by increased endorphins and adrenaline in your body. The sensations vary from person to person, as well as varying degrees of intensity. It can be brought on from impact play - flogging, caning, etc. to intense orgasmic release, which is what I believe you experienced. It can last from minutes to hours. Your experience lasted a couple of minutes. I've only been sitting here with you a minute or so. Drink some water. It will help clear your mind."

"Wow...so much I don't know."

"You'll learn, it just takes time," he chuckles.

Adjusting myself on his lap, I feel his swollen cock between my ass cheeks. My eyes drop to his gaze, lingering a moment before his hands cup my face and his lips devour mine. While our tongues explore each other, my hand strokes the bulging leather, as his hands stroke my ass.

I want him so bad...my sex is throbbing. I just had an earth shattering orgasm, but I'm going to die if he doesn't sink his cock in me...NOW!

His hands work my dress up around my waist and I'm working frantically to free his cock from the restraint of his leathers. Finally, I work the laces loose enough to free my delectable prize. Lifting his hips to help, I shimmy his pants down, all without breaking the connection of our mouths.

Derek pulls away, breaking the searing kiss.

Is there such a thing as a beautiful cock... clearly there is considering I'm staring at one. Oh my god...

His eyes find mine, searching for the answer to his unspoken question.

I have no idea what I'm getting myself into, but right now I could care less. I've always done 'the right thing'. Sure...I have a sassy mouth and like to have a good time, but I've always been responsible. Tonight... I'm gonna do things a little bit reckless.

I ease up onto my knees, straddling over Derek's lap, his cock resting against my abdomen. Finding his eyes, I extend my legs, allowing my sex to hover over the head of his thick cock. He grips his shaft, sheathing it before rubbing the head between my slit, coating it with my essence. I can't take the sensation any longer, I sink balls deep on his cock; a rumbling moan acknowledging my pleasure.

Gripping my hips, Derek immediately takes over; lifting me up, then pulling me down, meeting his thrusts. He unzips the front of my dress, exposing my breasts. His lips lock around my pebbled nub, gripping it with his teeth. A piercing pain at first, then he laves the pain away with flickering from his soft tongue.

"I love your tits...perfect sized nipples to suck and bite."

Loves my tits...I don't have any.

He begins pounding into my sex, grinding across my swollen clit. Pressure builds in my core, on the verge of erupting like a volcano. His fingers sink into my fleshy ass, squeezing as he pummels my pussy. Unwavering ecstasy...

"Shit... I'm gonna come, Sir."

A blistering slap lands on my ass. *What the hell???*

"Watch your mouth!"

"Oh, uh...Sorry... Sir, but I need to come. Please...I'm begging."

His response is continued thrusting with added pressure to my clit. *Aaahhh...I can't take it.* I feel his cock thicken, as his momentum slows. He pounds two more hard thrusts...

"COME NOW!!!" He roars and we both find our release.

****

So much for not having sex during a scene. Although, it was technically after the scene. Tie me up, blindfold me, and I'll let you fuck my brains out. Slut... yep, that's me. What does he think of me now?

After a tender kiss on my forehead, Derek begins cleaning the equipment while I pull myself together. I have a feeling I look like I've been rode hard and hung out to dry.

"What can I help you do?" I ask walking up behind him.

"I'm about finished sanitizing the chairs, so if you'll wipe down the cuffs and the Wartenberg Wheel and put them in my bag, we'll have it wrapped up."

"Wartenberg Wheel? What's that?"

Derek reaches across me, picking up something resembling some type of medical instrument. It's a six inch handle with a wheel of needle-like prongs at the top; made of stainless steel.

"This is the Wartenberg," rolling it along the underside of my forearm. "Do you recognize it, now," he offers with a devilish grin. A shiver radiates through my body from the feeling of this wicked tool.

Regaining my composure, the nagging feeling of needing to explain my behavior begins to consume me.

"I, um...I don't... I mean, haven't - ever done this before. What I'm trying to say is that I don't just have random sex. Honestly...I don't." The words tumble out of my mouth, in a desperate attempt to explain my slutty behavior.

A small chuckle rumbles from his chest. "I hold no thought that you do. I wouldn't have fucked you if I thought you did. I'm not a magician, I don't do *tricks,*" he smirks.

I'm a little slow to catch his play on words. Understanding dawning, a cackle explodes from my chest, tears pooling in my eyes.

"I've never heard that comeback before."

"You liked that, did ya?" He touts over my snuffling laughter.

"Pretty clever, Sir."

"Look, we're unattached, consenting adults. The opportunity presented itself and it felt good, felt right. I have no regrets...do you?"

"Regrets...me? Oh, no... I would do it again in a heartbeat," I declare enthusiastically, before getting control of my mouth. *Gawd...I sound so desperate.*

"Good to know...," he winks and blasts me with his devastating smile. "Let's go check out a few more scenes and then we can discuss my plans for the first class, next week."

****

Derek

What a stroke of luck! Walking into the bank that day and seeing Little Miss Submissive Sunshine. I couldn't have planned it better. However, sinking deep in her sweet pussy wasn't in the plans, especially this soon. Damn...she was so fucking responsive; I couldn't help myself. The Shibari classes could get very interesting.

"What's up Derek?" Patrick jars my thoughts.

"Hey man, what's going on tonight?"

"Nothing much. Late getting here...again. Working 14 hours a day is getting old. Damn criminals need to take a day off," he smirks. "Hey...that chick over there talking to Gina; were you scening with her earlier?"

"Yeah, that's Katherine's friend Debra. She's my new demo assistant for the rope classes."

"The sounds I heard coming from her, it seems to me like you were the one doing the assisting," Pat laughs.

"I'll assist that tight pussy anytime," I firmly acknowledge. "It wasn't my plan for tonight, though. My intention was for us just to familiarize ourselves with each other and her with Nexus. Oh well...they say the road to hell is paved with good intentions. No regrets, man."

Debra pivots her stance during her conversation with Gina; she's now facing us.

"Oh hell, I remember her. That's *Sunshine*," recognition dawns on Patrick. "I remember that sexy yellow dress."

I chuckle at Patrick's use of the same moniker for Debra I use. *Sunshine...*

"You're demoing rope on her for your classes, huh. Did Kathy hook you up?"

"Funny thing, I've been looking for someone to assist me, but I wanted it to be someone that I hadn't played with. I want the class to see realistic scenarios they will have to deal with, and the only way for that to happen is for the person I use in the demonstrations not to know me or my expectations. I hadn't even considered Debra because she didn't come to the club and honestly, she kinda fell off my radar. A couple weeks ago, I happened to run into her at the bank and remembered her from Open House. We went to lunch, talked, and she agreed to help out."

"Damn... you lucked out."

"Yeah, I did. Man... She's submissive, through and through; a diamond in the rough. We've talked a lot, but right now she's just committed to assisting with the classes. I mentioned the sub training program and it piqued her interest. Her body is so responsive. That's why I couldn't resist dipping in that sweetness tonight."

"How much do you know about her?" Patrick inquires, trying to be subtle, but failing. Clearly Debra's interest isn't the only one that's been piqued.

"She's single, been divorced for several years. Hell, I've met her ex."

"What? You're shittin'."

"Nope. He happened to be at the same restaurant the day we went to lunch. She wasn't too happy to see him. My first impression... he's a prick."

"Most exes are... Pricks or dicks," Patrick sneers his opinion. "Have you gone through the checklist with her?"

Shooting him my *'do I look like a dumbass'* look, "Of course,

I did. I don't play without it."

"And..."

"Her pertinent hard limits, that pertain to play here at Nexus - needles, blood play, breath play, and humiliation."

"Huh... So she's obviously okay with sex and play. What about..." Patrick trying to string his thoughts together.

What the hell is up with him? He's normally Mr. Calm, Cool, and Collected. Right now, he's as awkward as a virgin gettin' his first piece of ass.

"Pat, man... you got a thing for her?"

"What? Naw, man. Just curious..."

"Oh...right. Well to satisfy your *curiosity,* 'Multiple partners' was noted as her having no experience, but *interested.*"

The grin on Patrick's face needs no explanation, neither does mine.

CHAPTER 8

The painful urge to pee pulls me from my peaceful slumber. Yawning and stretching, I blink my eyes repeatedly, preparing them for the harsh morning light. Jeez, it's awfully bright this morning. Uncurling my arms from my pillow, I stretch again before turning toward the clock to sneak a peek...10:14. Holy shit...10:14!!! I haven't slept this late in years. I must've died when my head hit the pillow last night. It's been a while since I've had a good night's sleep.

Bladder relieved, I plop back in the bed, covering up to my ears. Snuggling my pillow, I close my eyes and the previous night's sinful events, begin to play through my mind. My sex begins to quiver as I'm reminiscing. That is, until the frame of turning and seeing Derek talking to Patrick, comes in my mind. *Their smoldering looks caused my breath to catch in my throat. I know they were talking about something concerning me, but I was too nervous to ask Derek about it on the drive home. Once again, Derek was a perfect gentleman, leaving me with a soft kiss on my cheek.*

After dozing back off, my elicit dream of me in bed with Derek...and Patrick, startles me awake. *What the hell...* Shortly after noon, I drag my lazy ass out of bed to face the day. *I may have to face the day, but I can face it in my jammies.*

Laundry started, I piddle around putting odds and ends back in their place. Not much to clean when you live alone. Making my Sunday call to mom, I'm surprised when she says Isaac sent a work crew down on Friday. I knew he said he would, but I didn't think it would be this quick.

"Debra, the room looks amazing. I just love it. Your daddy would be so happy. Those men worked so hard. They were here all day Friday and most of the day Saturday," Mom boasted.

"Hmm... It must have taken longer than Isaac thought to finish the sunroom."

"No, they finished the sunroom Friday, but then they built an awning to connect the backdoor to the carport. Now, I won't get wet when it rains when I go to and from the car."

"Really??? That was very thoughtful of them."

"That's not all. They reinforced the door jams, built some new handrails for the porch, and added a security system. If I fall or get sick...I push a button on my necklace and it will call 911 and call you. So cool..."

Cool???...Who the hell am I talking to??? My mom doesn't say - cool.

"Yeah, that's...*cool,* mom. How much was the bill? I'll pay for the repairs."

"They didn't give me a bill and wouldn't take any money. The man in charge, I think his name was Leo...yes, Leo, like a lion. He's a nice looking man, Debra."

"I'm sure he was, Mom." *She's still trying to find me a man.*

"Anyways, he said he would lose his job if I paid them money, Mom marveled.

"I'll talk to Kathy and find out how much it was. That's a lot of work and he should be paid."

"Yes... and I'll pay for it," Mom declares.

I'm not arguing with her. I'll get Kathy to ask Isaac for the price, I'll pay it, and Mom won't know the difference.

"I just hate Isaac didn't make it down. It would've been nice to see him again," Mom gushes.

I think Mom has a thing for Isaac... Damn cougar!

"I'm sure he was busy or he would've come down himself," I cajole her and giggle inside.

Phone call to Mom over and laundry complete, I settle on the sofa with my Kindle to recharge my battery for another week.

****

Monday drags into Tuesday, Tuesday into Wednesday. They can keep their *'Hump Day'*. I need a *'Wine Down Wednesday'*. Thank God, Kathy is coming back in town today and we're having dinner tonight. On Monday, she left for a business trip to Chicago. I haven't had a chance to talk to her about all the revelations I learned last weekend about Derek and Isaac, Derek and Patrick, and Derek, Isaac, and Patrick. Nor have I had the chance to discuss the pulverizing my pussy took from Derek's cock. Wrapping up and clearing my desk, I head out to meet Kathy at McGee's for dinner.

Settling into the booth, Kathy sneaks in and slides on the other side.

"Hey...how was your trip to Chicago?"

Kathy lets out a long sigh, "The business aspect was good, but I have to admit, I was a nervous wreck most of the time. The attack in Memphis replayed in my head, over and over. I couldn't sleep, being in the room alone. I moved, not one, but two chairs up against the hotel door, wedging the second one under the knob on the closet door. Thinking I was safer, until thoughts of a fire in the hotel caused me to second guess trapping myself in the room. My mind being at full on spazz mode, I began rationalizing the probability of a fire in the hotel versus someone breaking in the room. Finally, realization dawned on me; no one broke into my hotel room and attacked me in Memphis, I opened the fucking door and they walked on in."

"Oh Kathy, I can't imagine how you felt. I'm surprised Isaac didn't go with you...or keep you from going."

"Oh, believe me, he wanted to go. He had a meeting to present a new building proposal that he couldn't miss. He's tried very hard not to interfere with my job, but this trip had us both on edge. We kept the video chat on all night, while we tried to sleep. Isaac could see and hear me, I could see and hear him. It was the only comfort we had. The stress and tension's not worth it. Which is why I turned in my letter of resignation to AMG this afternoon," Kathy divulges, as she downs her glass of wine.

"WHAT?!?! Seriously...you're really leaving Atlanta Media?"

"I've been thinking about Isaac's offer to work for him full-time. I've teetered back and forth with the idea. I've worked at AMG over 14 years. I love my job. However, I can't go through all this anxiety every time I go out of town for business.

I was a little concerned about us working together 24/7. Then I began to think about how it's been working for him at Nexus and it's been great. He's allowed me to restructure the accounting system the way I wanted and he's not interfered. I know it will be different at the construction company, but I actually look forward to working with him to build a stronger company."

"I'm surprised, but you seem very confident and at peace with your decision. I'm so excited and happy for you. I'm sure Isaac is happy with your decision, too."

"Yes...he is. He's been an ornery ass the past week, leading up to my trip," she snickers. "I'm happy that's the last one I will go on alone."

"Hey, that reminds me. I know you're not working there, yet, but did you know Isaac sent a work crew down to Mom's last weekend?"

"Yeah, he wanted to go down, himself, but he was prepping for his meeting all weekend."

"Well, the foreman didn't leave a bill, so could you check with Isaac for me, to see how much Mom owes? I'm going to pay it for her."

"The bill's already been paid."

"No... Mom said she didn't get a bill, so I know it hasn't been paid, yet. God, I hope Mom isn't developing dementia. She said..." Kathy erupts into laughter interrupting my train of thought.

"Your mom doesn't have dementia," she blurts through her laughing fit. "Isaac took care of it. No worries..."

"No, no, no... oh my god, Kathy, he has to be paid."

"Ummm, you tell him that, 'cause... I'm not," she sasses, rolling her eyes.

"Kathy...do you have any idea how much work was done? He finished the sunroom, built an awning, and reinforced her doors. He can't do that for free."

"He can and he did. You won't change his mind, so just accept it. He wanted to do it, Deb. He really did. Do you honestly think Isaac Jameson does anything he doesn't want to? And furthermore, once he sets his mind to do something, no one is stopping him. Trust me..."

"He put in a freakin' hi-tech security system, too," I whisper shrill at her.

"Actually, I picked it out," she gushes. "He has a buddy that has a security monitoring company, so her monitoring is free, too."

"WHAT!?!"

"Pipe down! He was concerned about your mom being down there alone. He's protective, Deb. He said he would have done the same for his mom. I can call him and you can argue with him about it if you like, but I still have a sore ass from my own run-ins with challenging his protectiveness."

"Whatever... I sigh, knowing I'm defeated in this matter.

"So tell me... how'd it go with Derek last weekend?"

"Well...let me start by saying I'm a *ho.*"

Kathy erupts into laughter once again.

****

Should I eat now or wait 'til I get home??? I'm so nervous, my tummy is flip flopping. I don't want any bodily function fiascos at the first class tonight. I definitely don't want to embarrass Derek or myself. It's a no brainer...eat later.

I'm dressed like I'm going to the gym instead of a BDSM club; spandex tank top, shorts and sneakers. Derek said it would be best to be comfortable for the first few classes, as he would just be talking safety and demoing simple techniques.

My anxiety increases a bit when I pull into the parking lot as Nexus. This will be the first time I've seen Derek since our little rendezvous last weekend. I'm not sure how I'm supposed to act; nonchalant, like his delectable fucking meant nothing, or more affectionate and territorial.

I nearly jump out of my skin at the tapping on my window. In my immediate view, there's a thick cock neatly packaged in black leather. My gaze travels upwards and I'm rewarded with his gorgeously chiseled face, plump suckable lips, and warm chocolate eyes. *Derek Moore...*

He opens my car door and I step out, bringing me a breath away from his hard body. He leans back slightly, his eyes roving from my head, to my toes and back to my eyes. He leans down, brushing his lips to mine.

"I love you in yellow, Sunshine, but you are banging in this hot pink and black outfit. It fits your body like a glove," deepening his kiss.

We proceed into the club where we're greeted by Tiny. And just as is typical of others having that nickname bestowed upon them; standing at least six and a half feet tall and weighing over 400 pounds, Tiny is the epitome of irony. I could easily be mistaken for an oompa loompa when I stand next to him. *I would hate to piss him off...*

It's unusually quiet in here, but I guess we *are* kinda early. Zeke's leaning on the counter talking to a statue of sinful sexiness. *Who the hell is that???*

"Derek, my man...long time no see," the sinful god greets.

"Leo...I heard you were back. How've you been?"

Leo...Leo...Leo the lion. Oh my god... Mom does have a keen eye for men.

"I'm good...glad to be back in the states. I've had my fill of living the desert life."

"It's hard to trust what the media reports, so how bad is it?" Derek asks, his concern clearly evident on his face.

"It's getting pretty tense over there. The increase in terror attacks is why I'm back early. I wasn't due back for three months, but the company I contract through pulled us out. I'm not complaining though; I was ready to get the hell out of there."

"I'm sure Isaac's happy to have you back. From what I can tell, his business has exploded lately."

"Yeah, but he's obviously had time to find himself a woman," the sexy beast chuckles. "I thought he was bull shittin' when he told me he was getting married. Hell, I'm waiting for Earth to stop spinning, 'cause that's what I thought would happen before Isaac took the plunge again. He seems happy, though. I really like Kathy, well what I know of her. She must be a helluva woman to bring Isaac to heel."

"She is and she's perfect for him. He's the happiest I've ever seen him," Derek confirms.

I remain standing just behind and to the side of Derek; eyes bugging out and chin scraping the floor. *Where do all these sexy men come from??? I'm beginning to think Isaac has a human cloning machine here and he just manufactures all this hotness; adjusting the settings for variation.*

"Leo, this is Debra. She's a friend of Katherine's and new to Nexus. She's assisting me with the rope class. Debra, this is Leo, a longtime friend of Isaac."

Steele gray eyes settle on me. "Nice to meet you, Debra."

"And you as well, Leo," I reply, extending my hand to shake his.

"Alright, Sunshine...time to get set up for class. Good to have you back, Leo. We'll have to get together to catch up." Derek concludes the conversation, shaking the sex god's hand.

CHAPTER 9

Derek leads us down a hallway, passing several private theme rooms. We stop outside a room with a plaque on the door identifying it as a *classroom*. I assume it's another theme room, *hot teacher scenario comes to mind*, but I'm surprised to see tables, chairs, a whiteboard, and projector; a real classroom.

"Yeah, this is an actual classroom," Derek confirms, obviously recognizing the surprise on my face, startling me at the same time. "We do some of our training in here; submissive, master, and safety training, all take place here at the club. There's usually some note taking that needs to take place at the beginning of most of the training that we do."

It still amazes me all of the things that go on in this club. There's so much going on behind the scenes, no one really is aware of. I just imagined there was always just a bunch of sex going on in here. It never occurred to me there was a process or procedure that took place in order for the club to run like a fine oiled machine.

Derek begins unpacking his leather duffel bag. I watch as he meticulously lays out links of rope in varying sizes, diameter, and color. They're fairly short in length, obviously meant to be used just for training. They are roughly 3 feet long. I can't see where a piece of rope that length could completely bind someone. However, I don't think I will test that theory.

Idly, I began to gently stroke each link of rope. I'm surprised at how soft the rope feels; some of it feels as soft as satin. The image of coarse, prickly twine is replaced with braided silk. A clanking noise on the table catches my attention. I notice a very odd shaped pair of scissors; bent in the middle.

"What are these?" I ask, picking up the funny shaped scissors.

"They're EMT shears used for cutting rope. Riggers or rope tops, as they're sometimes called, must have a way to cut through the rope in an emergency. EMT shears, sailing knife, hook cutters; regardless of the device, it's imperative that it is readily available in the event of an emergency. They should also be tested to ensure their capability of cutting through the type of rope that's being used at the time," Derek explains.

"Should the person being bound witness this testing?"

"Great question, Sunshine. That depends on the rope bottom and their trust in the rigger. Most definitely if it's a new partner or if you would feel more comfortable."

"This is all very informative for me."

"Exactly the reason we have training," he grins.

****

Twelve people show up for the class. Most are coupled, but there are two individuals from what I can tell. Derek explains the importance of safety and descriptions of the safety devices, with extraordinary detail. I'm in awe of his oral skills. *Mmmmm...Yes, those oral skills, too, snickering to myself. I'd love to be experiencing those oral skills right now.*

Not much demonstrating tonight. He tied a few loops around my wrist, using the safety devices to cut them off; simulating an emergency.

Derek begins packing up while I wrap up collecting contact information from the group. I tidy up after they leave, waiting for Derek to finish. *Hmmm...I wonder if we're gonna play now.*

I check my email while I wait and notice a missed call from Scott and the voicemail icon is illuminated. I ponder the reason why Scott would be calling for a moment, before Derek derails my thoughts with a kiss to my forehead.

"Thank you for your help tonight and for suggesting I gather email addresses for correspondence with the group. I also like your idea about blogging the class information. I hadn't thought of documenting the class material that way. I'm not into social media much, so I could use your expertise."

"I'd be happy to help, Sir."

He takes my elbow and guides us back through the club. It's busier than I thought it would be. Several couples are cuddled up in the oversized chairs. A snapping sound cracks through the air, getting my attention and I slow to a halt. Tracing the direction of the sound, I discover the sex god I met earlier tonight, cracking a whip against an empty St. Andrews cross. Muscles ripple across his back with each strike. SEXY...but damn if I want to be on the receiving end of that whip. *Yikes...*

With a wicked grin, Derek nudges me along, passing through the dungeon area, around to the lobby area. *Uh...guess we're not playing tonight.*

"I'll walk you out to your car," Derek states, matter of factly.

"Oh...okay," I emote aloofness.

Derek escorts me to my car, while insecurity and self-doubt ooze through my body.

"I have to go to Augusta for a deposition tomorrow and I'll be late getting back. I'd like you to join me here Saturday night. That is...if you're free," he inquires.

"I don't have anything planned." *Damn girl, don't be such an eager beaver. Who am I kidding? I have a beaver, that's very eager.*

"Good, now you do," he replies kissing my fore head again. "Call me when you get home so I know you made it safely."

"Okay..." I numbly reply, unable to focus as my mind begins to race.

Settled in my car, I head home. *What the hell?!?!?! Kissed on the forehead. Twice... He gave me the most thorough fucking I've ever had a few days ago. And tonight -- nothing.*

Maybe I read too much into last weekend. Maybe it was just a casual fuck for him and nothing more. *Jeez... Slow your horses, Deb. Don't make a fool of yourself.*

****

Scott's been a little impatient. He's already called again this morning. It was too late to return his call last night. Once I got home and called Derek, I went to bed. I guess I'll call now, while there's a break in my schedule.

He answers on the first ring - anxious, aren't we.

"Hey Scott, what's going on? I see you've called a couple of times."

"Hey... How've you been, Deb?"

"Good. Thanks."

"Your mom? How's she doing?"

"She's doing really good. I'll tell her you asked. So, what's up? I know you didn't call twice to ask how I'm doing."

"Uh - no," his laughter fake. "I was going through some boxes I have in storage and came across the cuff links your dad let me borrow. I wore them to the charity ball we went to, years ago. Do you remember that?"

"Of course... It was a very elegant event." *Though, I've since suspected he had one of his elicit encounters that night; disappearing with a female associate to do some networking. At that time, I was proud of his business initiative, but after the discovery of his habitual adulterous behaviors, I've scrutinized every moment of our lives together - questioning every encounter.*

"I thought you may want them back, especially now."

"Yes - I would. Thank you."

"No thanks needed. So, if you're not busy, maybe we can meet for dinner tonight," he offers.

Dinner??? Tonight... I don't think so. After the incident at Mom's, I don't want to send any mixed messages.

"Actually... I'm busy tonight." *Liar...*

"Oh...okay. Well, I can come by..."

"What about coffee tomorrow afternoon?" I interrupt him. *No way I want him coming over to my place.* "At Mocha Joe's, around the corner from the bank. 2pm."

"Sounds good. See you then."

CHAPTER 10

Saturday morning cleaning complete and errands run, I decide to treat myself to a new outfit to wear to the club tonight. After a quick shower, I head out to do a little shopping before I meet Scott this afternoon. Kathy told me about a new adult novelty store across town. And that will be in the first stop.

The amazing variety in the store has kept me occupied and time has slipped away from me. I found an outfit as soon as I walked in, but I've been carrying it around with me while I checked out everything else. Though I've seen lots of beautiful clothes, I purchase the sinful ensemble I picked out initially; black pleather short shorts laced up in the back with a zippered crotch. Paired with a black pleather shelf bra that matches perfectly.

I sprint back across town to Mocha Joe's to meet Scott. I'm a little uneasy meeting him. The *incident* that happened at Mom's really makes me uncomfortable around Scott. I have a weird feeling meeting him today.

I walk in and see him sitting at a table in the back corner. I throw up my hand to wave and step up to the counter to order.

Caramel latte in hand, I nervously make my way to the table.

"Hey…" He greets me happily.

"Hey."

"You look great, Deb. Things must be going good for you."

"Thanks. Things are good. Hope they are for you. By the way, when's the wedding?"

"Uh, um – not sure."

"You are getting married, aren't you?"

"Oh, uh – yeah. Just haven't set a date."

"Oh, I see."

He appears pretty uncomfortable discussing his impending marriage. I'm not gonna press the issue, so I change the subject.

"Can I see the cuff links?"

"Sure – here you go."

An iron cross set in the center face of the cuff link, surrounded by an elegant filigree design. Two Fleur-de-lis are imprinted the on the back of the face, one on each side. The tubing that connects the back plate to the face of the cuff link, is imprinted with a replica of the intricate filigree design on the face. The Fleur-de-lis, a symbol of Dad's French heritage.

"Thank you for returning them to me. You never know how much someone's personal possessions will mean to you until they're gone. So, thank you,"

"They belong with you." A pregnant pause lingers before he continues. "One of my regrets in life is knowing how much I disappointed your dad and how much I hurt you with my reckless behavior. He trusted you, his only little girl, with me."

Where the hell is this coming from?

"Scott, is everything okay with you?"

"Yeah, I've just been thinking about my life and how I've fucked it up."

"You just have to learn from your mistakes. I'm sure you'll do things differently in your new marriage."

What the hell am I supposed to say? He's starting to wig me out.

"Deb, if I could go back and undo the shit I did that hurt you, I would. I'm so sorry."

"Unfortunately, we can't go back in time. We can only take what we've learned and move forward."

"It wasn't you, Deb. It was all me. You were a great wife. I was just too stupid to appreciate you," he reaches over and cups my hands.

Oh my god. I don't want to listen to this. I can't look at him with that 'come hither' look on his face.

"No need to rehash the past. That was six years ago and I think we've moved on successfully. *At least I thought we had. Now... I'm not so sure.* "Look, we're sitting here having coffee and I haven't killed you. Plus, you have all your body parts intact. I call that progress."

Jee-zus, I need to get out of here. He must be having a midlife crisis or something and I want no part of it.

"You're right," he chuckles.

"Well, I guess I better go. I've got some errands to run." *Liar – shit I'm gonna look like Pinocchio with all these little white lies.*

"Yeah, I need to go, too."

"Thanks again for the cuff links," I reply, standing to leave.

Scott slightly closes the gap between us, like he's leaning in for a hug or possibly a kiss. Something... He leaned in for something. Instinctively, I step back.

Stepping away, I turn back, "Take care, Scott."

****

Derek's on his way to pick me up. I'm feeling a little off. Between trying to understand the dynamics of my relationship with Derek and then Scott's mess this afternoon, I'm mentally pooped. I tried to take a nap when I got home from meeting Scott, but I was restless. The whole meeting was unnerving and set me on edge.

A soft knock of the door sends my heart strumming. Taking a deep breath, I open the door and drink up the deliciousness that stands before me.

"Hi...come in."

"Good evening, Sunshine." Derek's eyes peruse my body from head to toe; an incredulous look on his face. It takes a moment but I realize the reason for the confusing look on his face. It's from what I'm wearing; the belted shirt dress. *I can't go out wearing these shorts and bra and nothing else. It's too chilly out, not to mention the indecency.*

"Oh, no worries. I'm just wearing the dress for extra coverage and warmth until we get to Nexus.

"Gotcha!" He pipes, relief spreading across his face.

****

I head straight to the locker room to remove my dress and store it in a locker. I check myself in the mirror and gasp at how little I'm wearing. I must've lost my mind to consider walking out of here looking like this. *What was I thinking when I bought it? What the hell am I doing here?*

"What's the holdup, Sunshine?" Derek's voice travels through the locker room.

"Just adjusting my outfit. I'm on my way out."

"WOW – you look deliciously fuckable," he whispers across my lips. A shiver bolts straight to my sex.

He takes my hand and leads us toward the lounge area. We round the corner at the bar and that's when I see *him* sitting back in the corner. *Master Patrick...*

Forget the butterflies, a freaking hummingbird is wreaking havoc in my tummy, as Derek leads us directly toward Patrick. I begin to stutter step and Derek falls in behind me, nudging me along with his hands on my hips. There's no barrier to protect me from Patrick's penetrating stare. Oh dear heavens – his smoldering look sends a bolt of lightning to my core.

"Sunshine, long time no see. Have a seat," Patrick croons, pulling out the chair beside him.

Holy mother of Hotness...

Derek and Patrick exchange pleasantries and engage in some informal hand – shake, grip, bump – that guy shake.

Still frozen in place, Derek guides me into the chair and sits down in the one beside me.

"How are you enjoying Nexus? Is Derek treating you right?" Patrick chuckles.

"Oh, um – Yes. Master Derek is wonderful. He's taught me a lot."

"I'm sure he has," Patrick winks.

Embarrassment expands from my chest, enveloping my face with heat. Derek leans into me, with Patrick on the other side, encompassing me with an aura of tantalizing testosterone.

"So, how was the meeting with your ex this afternoon?" Derek states quizzically.

My head spins so fast and abruptly stops, that my eyes twirl around a few more times. *What the hell...*

The awkwardness of the afternoon chat with Scott comes flooding back.

"It was fine."

"Fine? Isn't that code for *I don't wanna talk about it?*" Patrick chimes in.

I whip my head in the opposite direction, giving Patrick the stink eye. *I don't want to discuss Scott with them."*

"Check the tone of that look, Sunshine. That look will get your ass blistered," Patrick scolds.

My face is flaming – part from embarrassment, part from being pissed.

"What look? What are you..."

"Careful..." Derek interrupts with raised brow.

I pause and reconsider where I am and who I'm sitting between. *But damn, I don't want to talk to them about Scott. I'm already wigged out about his behavior around me, lately.* I don't want to add to the awkwardness by talking to these two about him.

"I'm sorry, really I am. I'm just not used to being accountable to anyone about what I do or how I feel. Especially, when it concerns my ex."

"I know you're not officially in sub training, but I must have openness – complete transparency, in my relationships. I feel we're in a relationship. Do you?" Derek queries.

"Well...I, uh – honestly I'm not sure. I know how I feel, but I have a tendency to misread the actions of others."

Derek leans over, covering my lips with his. He wraps his hand in my hair, taking my head back as his tongue slips between my lips, deepening his kiss.

Exhilarating and possessive...

"Did I clear up any misunderstanding?" Derek asks, his lips hovering above mine.

"Crystal clear," I sigh.

"Good. Now back to my original question. How was your meeting?"

"It was okay. He returned the cuff links to me."

"Yeah – you told me that's why he wanted to meet. You just seem a tad on edge. You were like this when I picked you up earlier. Did he upset you this afternoon?"

Oh god... I do not want to talk about this with them.

"Look, Sunshine – if a Dom's sub is upset, he is upset. It's our responsibility to take care of our sub – physically, mentally, emotionally, and financially. Whatever is needed," Patrick adds.

Shit, both of them on my ass.

Rolling my eyes, I let out an exasperated sigh. A fist in my hair once again, only this time my face is tilted up toward Patrick's.

"The only time you roll your eyes at me is when my cock is balls deep in your pussy. And then they'll be rolling back in your head."

A bolt of electricity streaks straight to my clit, pulsing with need. "Yes sir. I'm sorry Pat - Master Patrick."

"So what happened today that has you itching to be bent over my knee?" Derek redirects my focus.

Taking a deep breath, I just let it flow –

"Scott was reminiscing a bit too much for my comfort level. He's not normally like that and it just freaked me out a bit."

"About?" Derek implores.

"Our marriage – his regrets and such. Maybe his impending marriage has him revisiting the mistakes he's made. I don't know..." I shake my head.

"Did he do anything inappropriate? Touch you?" Derek continues his cross examination, with a hint of growl.

"No, just the ooey gooey way he was talking made me uncomfortable. He's normally a jerk, so this alter ego of his, put me off kilter."

"It is kind of strange. Did you ask him about it?" Patrick pipes in.

"No... There's actually something that happened about a month ago."

After explaining with immense embarrassment, the incident with Scott after Dad's funeral, I'm wound tighter than a drum. However, I feel a little relieved to have it in the open. Derek and Patrick both agree with me that Scott's finally realizing how much he screwed up.

Derek rests his hands on my shoulders and whispers in my ear, "I think you need some help relaxing, Sunshine. Patrick has a little treat in store for you."

"Patrick?" I whisper, as Derek guides me to my feet.

"I'll be there too, baby."

Derek and Patrick lead the way down the corridor where the private rooms are located.

Stepping through the door was like stepping through a travel portal; exposed beams, wrought iron art on the walls, a smaller version of a St. Andrews cross in the corner-though no less intimidating with its solid wood frame and ornate iron work on each corner. As beautiful as the cross is, the room is filled with a gorgeous king size bed with wood and iron work, matching the cross. A beautiful Spanish style bedroom in red and black.

"You're a little overdressed, Sunshine," Derek croons.

Overdressed? This is the skimpiest thing I've ever worn. My lady bits are barely covered. And he wants me to undress in front of Patrick... Holy hell...

"T-T- Top or bottom?" I stammer.

"Both!" Patrick demands.

CHAPTER 11

I'm shivering, my naked body leaning against the cool polished wood, fitting perfectly between my hardened nipples. My heart is pounding with excited trepidation. Derek is weaving an intricate pattern along my wrists with silken jute, attaching it to the wrought iron design at the corner of the cross. He's repeating the process already completed on my ankles; a trail of nibbles and kisses paving the way from corner to corner. Wetness pools, seeping between my labia.

"The thud of the flogger is going to help you relax. Remember, your safewords -Yellow to slow down, Red – everything immediately stops," Patrick assures me.

"I'll be right here, baby," Derek murmurs in my left ear.

Immediately, I feel soft tendrils of some type of material. The scent leads me to believe it's leather, stroking up and down my back. It feels as soft as cotton.

The first lash lands just as Patrick described, a thud; taking my breath away. Just as my lungs fill with air once again, another thud lands across my right shoulder. This pattern continues, striking each hip in sequence.

The repetition increases along with the intensity; crisscrossing my body-left shoulder, right shoulder, left hip, right hip, left shoulder again. His rhythm quickly sets to a thundering pace.

The struggle to catch my breath between strikes yields to a soft, shallow breathing that calms my nerves. I'm in a tranquil, serene state. With closed eyes, I feel like I'm floating in a dream, but I feel Derek nearby.

A line of fire sears across my ass cheek and my eyes flash open. *Different, oh shit...*

Another line of fire lands across my other ass cheek. *What the hell!* I'm still somewhat dazed but try to focus my eyes on Derek, who's standing in front of me.

"Look at me. I'm here, Sunshine. That's a good girl."

Derek begins to say something to Patrick and I close my eyes again. The fire on my ass dissipates with more relaxing thuds. The fire ripples to my sex and it begins to throb.

Fire intermingles with the thuds for a while and my pussy is throbbing with need. The essence of my sex trickles down the inner part of my thighs. I've relaxed to the point of delirium; my knees buckle and the weight of my body is being held by my wrists.

I feel my body being carried and gently lowered. Instinctively, I nuzzle into the crook of a delicious smelling neck. I lumber for what seems like just a minute, but I have no concept of time at this point.

Slowly my senses begin to stir and I begin to realize this is not Derek. I force my eyes to open, blinking repeatedly to focus and determine whose lap I'm sitting in.

"There she is..."

Derek... That's Derek's voice. He's here.

Squirming and twisting to sit up, my effort is halted by an enormous bicep and forearm, fitting snuggly of around my upper body.

"Ssshhh... Just relax, Sunshine," Patrick murmurs across my forehead.

"What was that? It was different feelings, thud and sting," I try to string words together to form a thought.

"I used a flogger mostly. The sting was from the quirt."

A sudden rush of heat consumes me and I realize a blanket is draped over me. A sheen of perspiration immediately begins to form. *Damn hot flashes...*

"I'm hot." I try wiggling around, again.

"Mmmm...yes you are," Patrick croons in my ear.

"The blanket... please take off the blanket," I plea.

Instantly the warmth is removed, replaced by cool air, chilling the dampness on my skin. My nipples bead and harden.

"Yeah, we can do without the blanket," Patrick offers, tweaking my right nipple. Without releasing, he tugs and squeezes my nipple once more. The waning throb in my sex erupts with a vengeance.

Of my god... What am I doing? I'm allowing Patrick to explore my body freely, getting aroused, and wanting more. All in front of Derek-whom I thought I was in a relationship of sorts.

With adrenaline, I bolt upright, breaking the hold Patrick has on me physically and sexually.

"Derek... Sir, I'm sorry. I don't-"

"Ssshh – it's okay baby. Relax and enjoy." Derek's luscious lips devour mine, while Patrick resumes taunting my breast.

I feel like I'm being pulled under by a rip tide. I find the strength to push back away from Derek and Patrick ceases the tugging on my nipple. I search Derek's face for clarity of what's going on here.

"Do you want me Debra?" Derek asks with sultry eyes penetrating my soul.

"Yes, Sir. You know I do."

"Do you want Patrick?"

Oh shit... Trick question. What do I say? Yes... and they both deem me a whore. Or do I say no and they know I'm lying? God, I can't lie.

"Yes," I whisper, hanging my head in shame.

"Look at me, baby." Derek lifts my chin. "You can have us both, if that's what you want."

WHOA – WAIT – WHAT?!?!?!

"Uh...do you mean - ?" I stammer. "I-I-I've never, ever done this." *Oh my god.*

"We'll teach you. If it's what you want." Patrick leans forward whispering in my ear.

"Um, I, uh – You've done this before? You two – together?"

"Let me clear some confusion. NO, not *us* together. Neither of us are gay or bisexual. However, on occasion, we have shared women and found we enjoy doing so," Derek explains.

"We've never been attracted to the same woman, and at the same time, the woman be open to this type of relationship. There's always been some part of the puzzle piece missing," Patrick adds.

"How do you know it will work with me?"

"We don't. But we're both very attracted to you. Your limit list has multiple partners as *interested*, so we thought we would see if you wanted to give it a try," Patrick continues.

Oh shit, oh shit, oh shit... What in the hell??? I'm 46 years old and the chance to have not one, but two sinfully sexy men fuck me.

"It's okay if you don't want to. We understand the complexity of a decision like this and the ramification it can have in your life," Derek interrupts my thoughts.

Ramifications. Yeah, I'm sure there would be some, especially if it lasted. But I'm tired of living my life to everyone else's standards. I want to live my life for me for change.

I lean forward, cupping Derek's face with both of my hands, gently covering his lips with mine. His lips part, inviting my tongue to explore. I move one hand away from Derek's face and reach back in search of Patrick's. I gently pull away from Derek's lips and turn back toward Patrick. Accepting my invitation, Patrick devours my mouth with his, as Derek laves my breasts and hardened nipples; sucking and nipping them.

I feel a finger, someone's finger, slip between my drenched folds. *Damn, I don't even know which one is dipping his finger in my sex.*

"Damn baby, you're so wet." *- Derek…*

Funny thing – before Derek, I needed a lubricant for sex. I thought I'd hit that 'age', when my own natural lubricant wasn't working as well. Sex was a little painful without the store bought kind. Derek quickly dispelled those thoughts. I'm like a freakin' waterfall with him and apparently Patrick has the same effect.

Derek shifts away from my breasts, opening my legs. A sucking sound draws my attention away from the mesmerizing kiss Patrick has me entangled with.

"You taste so fucking good – spicy sweet," Derek utters, licking his finger. "I need a better taste of my pussy."

His tongue delves between the swollen lips of my sex.

"Oh Sir – that feels so good."

Licking, sucking, biting every inch of my sex. I'm trembling with need.

Patrick has shifted and he's gripping the beaded nub of my breasts with his teeth. Pulling, elongating my nipple with a piercing pain before caressing it with his soft tongue. As he's caressing,

Derek's gripping my clit sucking it between his lips. Now Derek caresses and licks my clit softly, as Patrick nips and pulls. Vice versa, to and fro– on and on.

"OH MY GOD, I'm gonna come!" I screech.

"Go ahead baby, no restrictions tonight. Come all you want," Patrick growls.

"Coat my tongue with your juice, baby."

"D-man, I need a taste of her sweet pussy."

Derek reaches up and spreads wetness – my wetness, around my nipple. Patrick sucks my breast, moaning his pleasure.

I've never understood a man's attraction and need to taste a woman. My thought must show my face, as Derek again removes his fingers from my sex and reaches up my body.

"Have you ever tasted yourself, Sunshine?" He asks, coating my lips with my own essence. "Go ahead...taste."

Timidly, I stroke the tip of my tongue across the center of my bottom lip. *Kind of pungent and sweet.* Regardless of the taste, the sensualism involved in the act sweetens the experience.

Patrick wastes no more time before ravaging my mouth. *Oh my god – it's an erotic high, tasting myself on his lips.*

Derek inserts a finger as he continues sucking on my clit. His finger brushes across a spot inside that nearly catapults me off the

sofa. That, in combination with the sucking, biting, and licking of every erogenous part of my body, sends me over the edge and I scream and shudder my release.

My recoup time is zilch, as Patrick gathers me in his arms, carrying me over to the bed. He positions me across the center of the bed. Derek is on the opposite side and he gathers me under my shoulders, pulling me toward him.

My head dangles slightly off the edge of the bed, with Derek hovering above me. Holy shit... He's stroking his cock that's on display. He has the most beautiful cock I've ever seen. The coloring is perfect.

"I want to fuck that pretty mouth of yours, Sunshine."

Holy hell – a beautifully thick fudgesicle. Yum!

"I'm gonna tilt your head back slightly and make it easier for you to take most of my cock without gagging."

My head is slightly upside down and he's supporting my neck. I lick my lips as the head of his cock nears my mouth.

"That's a good girl. Wet them lips for your Master's cock."

My sex is pulsating in anticipation. When the head gets close enough, I glide the tip of my tongue through the slit, lapping up the salty drop. A moan escapes from him as he glides his cock between my lips. He eases in and out, gaining more entrance with each gentle pump.

God, this is amazing. He's at the back of my throat and no gagging. His thrusts increase and I relax the back of my throat and jaw, even more.

"Mmmmm..."

"Yeah, that's my girl. I fucking love it when you moan around my cock."

The bed dips slightly and my legs are being repositioned; knees bent up and spread apart. I feel Patrick place the head of his cock between my sodden folds. He moves it up and down between my slit massaging the head across my clit. *It's driving me insane.* All I can do is let out a long moan.

"Fuuuck," Derek groans. "Man keep that shit up. Keep her moaning across my dick." Derek's hand palms my breast, kneading and pulling and tugging.

Derek glides his finger across my cheek and gently pulls out. Patrick grabs my hips and pulls me back to the center of the bed. Before I can collect my thoughts, he drives balls deep into my sex.

"Aaaaahhhh..." I shrill.

Patrick thrusts deep in my core. He tilts my hips slightly and drives even deeper. I've never felt so full. Derek leans over, flicking his tongue across my nipple before gripping it between his teeth. My body is so hypersensitive; I feel like I'm going to combust. But it feels absolutely amazing. I'm on the verge of exploding.

Patrick thrusts come to an abrupt halt.

"No, no, no… Oh my god. I need to come. Please!"

Patrick ignores my plea and flips me over, burying his cock balls deep again. He begins a pounding rhythm. Derek makes his way onto the bed, slipping his cock between my lips once again. They soon find a smooth, alternating rhythm that sends me soaring.

After a few deep thrusts from each of them, Patrick reaches around and squeezes my clit. Unable to control myself any longer, I wail an indecipherable sound and shatter beneath them. Patrick thrusts once more before roaring his own release, as Derek finds his.

Cuddled up between these two deviantly, delicious men, I can't help but think I'm dreaming. *What do they see in me? I'm in my mid-forties. Eight years older than either of them. God, what have I gotten myself into?*

"So – what can we three be for Halloween?" Patrick disrupts the realm of quiescence.

"Halloween?" I ask befuddled.

"Yeah, we'll need costumes for the annual Halloween party at Nexus."

"Oh..."

CHAPTER 12

Isaac and Katherine

"Good morning, J & J Contractors. I'm sorry, Mr. Jameson's not in. May I take a message?"

I'm still not used to saying *Mr. Jameson*. Thankfully, most of his calls are informal. As nervous as I was to give up my career at Atlanta Media, I feel totally at peace with my decision to join Isaac, working at his construction company, as well as continuing to work at Nexus.

I'm still blown away that he's given me carte blanche to revamp the accounting system and procedures. Owning two businesses that are distinctively different, requires careful accounting. Currently, he has a good system for Nexus and one for the construction company. The problem is, they're two separate systems, requiring different sets of procedures.

Being that I'm now in charge of both systems, I want to streamline them to make it more effective. One of the first things I accomplished when I went to work at Nexus, was updating the bookkeeping and files. I really like how that system works, so I chose an optimized version of that software to use for the construction company.

The electronic bell on the front door rings and a cute, nerdy *Dean Cain* version of Clark Kent, steps into the lobby.

"Hi, I'm looking for Ms. Stevens."

"Hey, that's me, but please, call me Katherine," I reply extending my hand.

"Katherine... I'm Pete and I'm here to install your new software."

After a few minutes of getting Pete settled in, I retreat to Isaac's office to work. However, the system's down for the installation, so I decide to do a little planning for the Halloween party.

The morning flies by, but I get a lot of planning for the party taken care of. I step of the office to check on Pete, the tech guy.

"How's it going?"

"Perfect timing Ms. Stevens. Installation is complete. So if you're free, we can get started on the training and transferring files."

"Great, let's get started."

A couple hours pass and we're making good progress on the files. My eyes are burning and I reach up to rub them both, knowing I will look like a raccoon afterwards.

"We can take a break, if you want," the tech guy offers.

"Yeah – I think she needs one," *his* voice rumbles.

"Hey babe, I didn't hear you come in," I acknowledge while excusing myself past Pete, the tech guy, to greet my man properly.

"I can tell," Isaac grouses, with a hint of darkness in his eyes. I reach up on my tippy toes and place a kiss on his soft lips.

Regretfully ending my kiss, I make introductions and Isaac heads into his office and I get back to training.

The number of times Isaac has passed back and forth by my desk, hasn't been lost on me.

"How much longer is this gonna take?" Isaac grumbles, stopping at my desk on his fifth pass by.

Why's he so grumpy?

"We're finishing up now, Mr. Jameson. Ms. Stevens is transferring the last few files."

"Please, call me Katherine. Mrs. Stevens was my mom," I chuckle.

"You can call her Mrs. Jameson. That will be her name very

soon," Isaac snaps, as he walks into his office. *Ooohhh...I see the issue now.*

Pete the tech guy, looks like he's been smacked upside his head by a grizzly bear.

"Thank you for all your help today, Pete." I try to soothe the verbal abrasion left by Isaac's tone.

Once Pete is out the door, I head to Isaac's office. Empty. *He must be in the shop.*

I settle in behind his desk to make the few updates and conversions to his computer. A hand grips in my hair and my head is tilted back slightly.

"I don't like other men hovering around what's mine," Isaac whispers harshly in my ear, then nips the bottom of my jaw.

"It was unavoidable, Sir. The position of my desk and being so close to the wall, it didn't allow much room to work," knowing exactly what he was referring to. *He didn't like the tech guy leaning over my shoulder.*

"I don't give a fuck."

"Oh Sir..., I'm old enough to be his mom."

A little tug on his grip guides me to my feet. He releases the grip in my hair, gripping my chin with his thumb and forefinger.

"I know he took every opportunity to get a peek at these beautiful tits," he states in his blunt manner, tweaking my nipple for punctuation. A different grip tightens in my core.

"He's just a kid," I mutter, trying to lighten his mood.

"He's got a dick - he likes tits and ass. Even guys playing for the home team like tits and ass."

I struggle to keep from bursting with laughter. But somehow I don't think he would reciprocate the emotion.

"These are my tits and my ass," he continues grabbing a handful of my ass. "I don't want men gawking at them, especially right under my nose."

Scorching heat radiates across the cheek of my ass from his open palm.

"Shit!" I cry out.

Another blistering sting connects with the other cheek.

"Watch your mouth!"

"I'm sorry Sir, but jeez – it hurts."

"I promise you – not as much as it could have," he sneers with a wicked gleam. "Now, bend across the desk."

For preservation of my ass, I quickly bend over, across his desk. He flips my skirt up and over to rest on my back. His calloused hands rubbing my ass, is like striking flint to stone. The abrasion igniting a fire to my sex. A couple more strikes to each cheek, followed by circular, calloused caresses, radiates molten heat to my core.

"My ass...," he growls. "My fuckin' ass."

His fingers grace through my slicken folds, delving deep.

"My pussy's wet for me. You like me spankin' that ass, don't ya?"

"Mmmm, yes," I moan, as he begins massaging my wetness around my clit.

A grumble escapes me when he removes his fingers from my sex and releases the slight pressure on my clit. The fire in my core flares when he smacks my reddened ass, again.

"Who are you growlin' at, Peaches?"

"I'm sorry, Sir, but damn it feels so good." An open palm to each cheek, continues dousing the flame.

"Do you need a gag for that mouth?"

"N-No, Sir," I stammer.

The fire disperses to my sex again, with a gentle caressing of both cheeks. With his hands still on my ass, and he pulls the rounded globes slightly apart, opening me up to him completely.

The tip of his tongue begins to tease and tantalize my clit.

A small quiver erupts at the epicenter of his touch, gaining momentum and quickly spreading. My legs are trembling with need. Thankfully I have the support of the desk under me because my legs are a quivering mess. He flattens out his tongue licking a path from my clit to my taut hole and back again. I'm grasping for the edge of the desk, sending his desk organizer crashing to the floor.

His tongue fucking abruptly stops and I'm left whimpering in its wake. My whimpers cease at the subtle sound of Isaac's zipper being lowered, replaced with a wanton moan. Isaac drives balls deep on the first thrust, a shrill of pleasure ripping from my throat; my arm stiffening and lifting my chest of the desk.

"This is my pussy," he growls into my neck. He bites my upper shoulder sending jolts of electricity straight to my clit.

He pauses a moment for me to adjust to him before setting his pounding rhythm. His balls slapping my ass cheeks with every thrust. This is Isaac's signature *possessive fuck*; marking his territory.

"Damn baby… You're so fuckin' tight. I love how you lock my pussy down on me."

I can't formulate a thought in my head. My only response to him is a whispering moan. He pulls my shoulders back just a bit, where I'm slightly bent at the waist. His thrusts continue, only now he's stroking that sweet little spot just inside my sex. The unique spot that shatters me.

"Oh my god, I'm gonna come – I *need* to come, please."

"Come for me baby. Cover my cock with your sweet nectar."

He hones in on that one spot – the spot that sends me soaring. My body is trembling and I tighten my white-knuckle grip on the desk and scream my release.

"That's my girl," he says slowing his rhythm, but not stopping.

The respite is short lived as he finds his pounding rhythm again.

"I know you have more for me, Peaches. I want it all. Give me everything. You belong to me," punctuating each word with a pulverizing thrust.

He knows my body so well. He plays it like a fine tuned instrument. He hovers around that deliciously, mystical spot. Teasing, stroking, and eliciting mewling sounds from me. He shifts slightly and adjust my hips, his pummeling cadence begins driving me to dizzying heights.

"I want you to drown my cock in your juices, baby. I want it dripping off my balls."

Oh my god, oh my god, oh my god...

Isaac reaches around and pinches my clit. White fire flashes behind my eyes and a dam-breaking explosion occurs.

"Fuck baby – my pussy's drenched, flowing all over me. Damn, you feel so good, baby," he moans, gripping my hips.

He slides his cock all the way out, then drives all the way in. He stills...motionless. He pulls all the way out and drives in again. He stills. Pulls all the way out...continuing his purposeful thrusts. I feel him begin to thicken inside me. He hammers two short, quick thrusts...and ROARS!

Feeling his pulsating cock inside me, reverberates another delicious orgasm for me.

I'm thankful for a bathroom in his office that also has a shower. The wetness oozing down to my knees would make for a sticky rest of the day. Emerging from the bathroom, I notice Isaac straightening his desk backup.

"I'll get the cleaner and wipe down your desk," I offer.

"No cleaner on my desk."

"Honey, I just came all over your desk."

"Exactly why you're not cleaning it. Why the hell do I want to smell lemons on my desk, when I have the sweet smell of my pussy on it?" He leans down and takes a long whiff of his desk. "Yep – my pussy."

I giggle and roll my eyes at his display.

Isaac takes my hand and pulls me down onto his lap on the sofa. "I think it's time, baby," Isaac moans into my hair.

"Time for???" I shuffle around to see his face.

"Time to get married."

"I thought we were waiting until after the beginning of the year, when business slows down for Winter."

"I don't want to wait. Business doesn't slow enough to affect when we get married. Besides, it's kind of a yucky time of year, weather wise."

"Well if you're waiting for nice weather, we'll have to wait for Spring. That's even longer."

"Spring? Why Spring? I thought you loved Fall," he states quizzically.

"I do. It's my favorite time of the year."

"So let's get married in the Fall."

I look at him like he has three heads, clearly not following his thought process.

"I mean, let's get married now."

"Now? Like elope?"

"No, I eloped the first time and didn't care. You deserve a wedding. We had a collaring ceremony and we'll have a wedding ceremony. By now, I mean in the next few weeks."

"Honey, there's no way we can plan a wedding in a few weeks. Unless we have a small ceremony at Nexus or our house," I explain.

"The collaring ceremony was at Nexus. Our house is connected to Nexus. I want the wedding somewhere else."

Obviously, he's been thinking about this.

"Okay, but we will be hard pressed to find a place on such short notice."

"Actually, I already have a place in mine and it's available – November 22nd," he says hesitantly.

"November 22… I guess you have been thinking about this a while."

He pauses a few seconds before answering, seemingly to gather his thoughts. "I have been thinking about it. I had an idea and wanted to make sure it would work before I mentioned it to you. Is November too soon? Do you need more time to think about it?" He asks cautiously.

"Oh no… Baby, I would marry you today. I know business is booming and you're very busy. I just didn't want to add the stress of planning a wedding with everything you have going on.

He cups my face with both hands, looking deep into my soul, "Baby, there is nothing more important in my world than you. Don't you ever doubt that," ending with a soft kiss on my lips.

"So where are we getting married?" I ask excitedly.

"Well, I really want it to be a surprise."

"A surprise?"

"I know it sounds kinda crazy and a little unorthodox, but this is something I want to do for you. I didn't want a wedding the first time and frankly never understood the hoopla surrounding one. That is, until I met you. I want to show you off and let the world know you are mine. I want your day to be as beautiful as you are to me. I know I'm asking a lot from you – entrusting our wedding day to me. But I promise, you won't regret it."

The tears that have pooled in my eyes begin to overflow and stream down my cheeks.

"Baby, why are you crying? If I'm asking too much, we can work it out. Please don't cry..."

Sniffling and wiping my eyes, I tried to regain my composure. "No, it's not that at all. I'm just so happy and can't believe you want to do this for me. I still can't believe how much you love me."

"I'm gonna spend the rest of my life proving it to you, Peaches," he whispers across my lips. "All you need to do is pick out your dress and leave the rest to me."

CHAPTER 13

I'm not a huge fan of shopping, but this is no ordinary shopping day. We are on the hunt for Kathy's wedding dress.

Kathy and I have been friends since college, since before she got married the first time. She didn't exactly elope the first time around, but she got married at her parents' house with none of the normal wedding fanfare.

We shared this special shopping day for my wedding dress when I married Scott, so I'm thrilled to get a second chance to have this special day for her.

Kathy likes shopping less than I do. The best thing about her shopping skills is the fact she knows what she likes and what she doesn't. One stop, though it's at a bridal outlet, is all it takes. Ten minutes in and she finds *the* dress. The sales lady helping us insists that she search for at least two more dresses to try on, for comparison. Kathy snags the next two dresses she finds in her size and we head to the dressing area. Kathy tries on the one she wants first, and that's all it takes.

She is stunning. Isaac will be wiping the drool off his chin. A strapless, mermaid style dress, in soft Champaign satin with lace overlay, snugging every curve.

Kathy doesn't waste her time trying on the other dresses. She gets her measurements for alterations, pays for the dress, and we're on our way.

It's a beautiful fall day so we decide to have lunch outside at Marietta Square.

"I just have to say again how beautiful you look in that dress. Isaac's going to love it. I'll be surprised if he doesn't have you out of the dress before you cut the cake," I giggle.

"Speaking of Isaac... I know you can't really tell me anything, but are the plans coming together for the wedding?" Kathy asks hesitantly.

I remember Isaac stopping by the rope class a couple weeks ago, asking me to stop by his office before I left. My damn tummy started flip flopping. It's like being called to the principal's office. *Well, he is the headmaster.*

Isaac shared with me that he would be planning his and Kathy's wedding and that it would be a surprise for her. It softens Isaac's hard edge in my eyes and made me cry happy tears. However, he made it very clear he didn't want Kathy knowing anything, so he would need my help with addresses for invitations and such. *So if this chick thinks I'm going tell her anything and have Isaac on my ass, she is sadly mistaken.*

"I really don't know much." *Which is not a lie – I really don't.* "Isaac is keeping it all pretty hush hush."

"I'm not surprised. I was told if I went snooping around, I wouldn't sit down until our first anniversary."

I howl with laughter, not doubting for a minute he would follow through.

"Thank you for taking the day off to go shopping with me. I'm glad we could avoid the weekend crowds."

"Girl, you know there's nowhere else I'd rather be. I'm so very happy for you! I haven't seen you this happy in – well, I've never seen you this happy."

"Well, you look pretty happy yourself. Things must be going good with your delicious duo."

"Things are going great."

"Girl, I can't even fathom being you – caught in their web of a wickedness."

"We're still testing the waters, and obviously have a lot to learn about each other, especially me. But they're so patient with me, answering my questions, teaching me about this lifestyle, and lenient with their expectations of me.

But to be honest Kathy, I still can't believe I'm having a relationship – having sex, with two men. It's been exhilarating and my eyes have been open to so much. However, it obviously goes against everything I was taught growing up, moral values instilled in me by my parents. But I've always followed the rules, done what was expected of me and look where it got me... 46, divorced, and alone. I don't know where this – this arrangement with Derek and Patrick will lead, but I'll never know unless I give it a try."

"Well, I certainly don't know anything about ménage and such, but I do know happiness. You look happy. And to me, that's all that matters."

****

Halloween – A Wicked Night of Heroes and Villains

The theme for the Halloween party is superheroes and villains, so I thought and googled what the three of us could dress up as and still be connected as a trio. Derek and Patrick wanted this as much as I did. There are many superhero couples, but no trios.

During my research, I continued to come across a triangular connection of sorts. On many lists of favorite superhero couples, Wonder Woman and Superman were listed, as well as Wonder Woman and Batman. I presented by findings to Derek and Patrick and it was settled.

Derek's wearing black, shiny, faux latex pants, which accentuates every curve and appendage of his lower half. A black mask that partially covers his face, with a black cape extending down his back, completes his look. He is Batman.

Patrick's wearing the same pants as Derek, only in royal blue. He's wearing a red cape and the trademark red **S** painted in the center of his chest. Superman... The view of them in those sinful pants causes wetness to trickle down my inner thigh.

I'm wearing a red satin bustier with gold lemme accents around the bust and a gold cincher belt; accompanied with a blue T-bar thong with white stars. Gold wrists cuffs and a headband complete my look – Wonder Woman.

Tiny meets us at the door and I'm momentarily at a loss for who he's dressed as. The caged mask across his mouth brings Hannibal Lector to mind. My pause lingers and Tiny answers my nonverbal question.

"I'm Bane from Batman."

"Ah – Gotcha. Guess I need to catch up on Batman," I chuckle.

Derek and Tiny spout off an exchange of character infused banter before we continue around to the lobby. Gina's standing behind the counter. Platinum blonde hair pulled up in pigtails, one dipped in red, the other in black.

"Oh my gosh, Gina, you look hot! Step back and let me see the head to toe look," I gush.

Gina's wearing a short, red and black bustier showing her midriff, paired with a white short-short skirt with red piping around the bottom. Red, Jester style thigh-highs play peekaboo above black thigh-high boots.

While I'm ogling Gina's outfit, I'm completely oblivious to the arrival of the *Joker* at the counter. I'm trying not to stare, but I can't figure out who it is. He hasn't said anything, so no help from his voice for recognition; just a creepy look in his eyes. A shiver streaks down my spine. *He's scaring the crap out of me.* I turn my attention back to Gina.

She is clearly affected by the presence of the *Joker*. Her eyes are wide and she's trying to be inconspicuous with her glimpses of him. *Obviously, Gina knows who the Joker is.*

"So Gina, who are you?" I ask.

"I'm Harley Quinn – from the Batman series."

"Oh, I'm not familiar with her." *I need to binge on some Batman to get caught up with all these new characters.*

"She belongs to me," the Joker interjects into the conversation.

I catch the noticeable hitch in Gina's breathing at the

declaration. Now my mind is spinning, trying to decipher what is going on between these two. Does he mean literally, figuratively, or by way of a TV show??? And, who the hell *is* the *Joker*??? His voice was no help to me.

"Man, I didn't even recognize you, Leo," Patrick concedes.

Leo – Oh... Now my curiosity is piqued.

I sneak a peek at Gina. She has her gaze on the floor, as Leo slowly pulls his away from her to respond to Patrick.

"Good, I don't want people knowing what they're in for."

I don't believe his cryptic response is necessarily meant to be a reply for Patrick, as much as a message to Gina. Another shiver slithers down my spine. If anyone in this club intimidates me as much as Isaac, it's this guy – Leo.

The door to the office opens and out comes nothing short of a vixen. She looks like she's been dipped in black liquid latex, the way her body suit clings to every curve. It's peeled away at the chest, showcasing her supple breast. Long, platinum blonde hair with black diamond shapes outlining her eyes that connect across the bridge of her nose, forming a mask. WOW – she is HOT!!!

"Kathy... Is that you?" I ask dumbfounded.

"Prrrrr... Tis me, love," she purrs in a sexy voice.

"You look A –mazing!"

"Yes she does," Isaac croons, smacking her ass. "I think this outfit adds a little sting to that ass when I smack it. I'll keep that in mind for later tonight."

The color briefly leaves Kathy's face at Isaac's suggested threat. And holy hell... Spiderman wishes he was as hulking as Isaac is representing him tonight. *Damn, we need to make these sexy, shiny, latex pants, part of the dress code for the Masters.*

"You look pretty wicked hot yourself, Wonder Woman," Kathy eyes me up and down.

"Wicked it is the word of the night," Derek announces with a devilish smirk. And heat flows straight to my sex.

Kathy and Isaac join us in the lounge area, near the bar. Zeke is the epitome of the All-American guy, so it's quite fitting that he is Captain America. A very sexy one at that. Seeing the string of women lined up at the bar, it's apparent my opinion is shared by many.

"Tainted Love" is synthesizing in the background. Marilyn Manson's version, rather than Soft Cell's. The dance floor is packed. An array of scantily clad superheroes and villains; bodies entwined.

"Hey Alexandria. It looks pretty busy at the bar," I tap her hand as she's whizzing by. "You look super-hot, girlie. I wish I had your long legs and figure," I muse.

A stinging swat lands on the side of my ass cheek. "Watch

your mouth, Sunshine. Sounds to me like you're speaking negatively about yourself and that's unacceptable," Patrick admonishes, while he soothes the fire in my ass with his hand.

"I'm sorry Sirs. I will work on my mouth and controlling what comes out of it."

"See that you do," Derek quips. "Now, let's dance."

****

After bumping and grinding between these two smoldering bodies, dampness has spread between my thighs. Thanks to the snug fit of their costumes, their rigid cocks are on display. *My god, I love running my hands over the silk material outlining their prominent manhood.*

The three of us begin to stroll around the club, checking out the scenes. My Sirs have just informed me, we would not be scening here. They have something planned for when we get back to my place. My anticipation ramps up, with a hint of trepidation.

We pause to watch Charlotte and Edward, aka Cyclops and Emma Frost. Ever since I saw the erotic debauchery these two displayed in the club a while back, my sex begins to throb whenever I'm around them. *I'm a twisted bitch.*

We don't linger at the scene with Charlotte and Edward, but continue around the open dungeon area checking everything out. I'm still awestruck watching the incredibly intimate activities that go on here. I find myself getting aroused when I do observe others. *I think I'm a closet voyeur.*

In the back corner of the open space, I see Isaac standing with his back to us. We wander a little closer and I see that he's standing in front of a large woven web, about 6 feet in diameter. Very apropos for Spiderman.

A closer look reveals Kathy strapped across the center, the top half of her costume removed, as well as the crotch, exposing her mons.

Isaac is flogging Kathy's breast. The falls of the flogger spread across her breasts when they land. After a few strikes, he switches to a miniature crop, approximately 12 inches long. He flicks it several times across her mound. My attention is drawn to the area where the soft end of the crop is striking and that's when I notice something on her mons. I step closer to gain a better look. I know I must look like a crazy person staring at her hooch, but I can't tell what's on it. *Oh shit, it's a tattoo. Kathy's got a freakin' tattoo on her hooch.*

"What's got you mesmerized?" Patrick whispers in my ear.

"Um... I think Kathy has a tattoo. I'm trying to see what it is," I whisper back, trying not to disturb Isaac. A couple more flicks and Isaac turns toward me.

"It's my initial – a brand. An early wedding gift to me. She got it early, so it would be healed before the wedding," Isaac responds, obviously overhearing my question.

Isaac steps over and I sidle up even closer to get a peek. It's a beautifully script *I*, with a heart dangling at the end. *Yep, we have some talking to do, me and Kathy.*

Kathy opens her eyes and sees me staring at her sex. I give her the two-finger point from my eyes to hers, letting her know that I see her tat and we're gonna be talking about it.

Patrick smacks my ass lightly and nudges me to move.

"Our night still awaits us. It's time to go," Derek adds a verbal directive to Patrick's physical one.

CHAPTER 14

"Present yourself," Patrick commands.

My presentation for them is standing nude, with my gaze to the floor, hands by my side. This is different from the normal kneeling posture, but both Sirs are well over 6 feet and tower over my short stature, as it is.

I quickly undress and lower my eyes in submissive respect. There's shuffling around in my bedroom, so I assume they are disrobing, too. I hear the bathroom door open, but I remain with my focus on the floor.

I feel some one step behind me, reaching around and palming my right breast. I steal a quick glance and see the beautiful contrast of color – Derek. I remain as still as possible, as he begins to knead my breast while he nibbles in the curve of my neck.

"Beautiful Sunshine," he murmurs across my skin.

A finger under my chin lifts my face and I meet Patrick's

eyes. He leans down and covers my mouth with his. His lips partially open in an invitation, so I gently caress his lips with the tip of my tongue. He nips my tongue and plunges his between my lips, delving in, plundering, and exploring. His hand grips in my hair, deepening the kiss.

Derek's hand leaves my right breast, traveling down to my mound. He glides his finger through the dewy petals of my sex. His other hand resumes massaging my left breast, elongating my nipple.

Tonguing, hair pulling, pinching, massaging, biting, and fingering – my god, I don't know how much more stimulation my body can take. My head drops back on to Derek's shoulder and I lose myself in the delirium.

My body is moving and I'm being lowered to the bed. The mattress dips on one side and then the other. The movement stirs me and I'm slightly more alert to my surroundings. The tantalizing ministrations of my body continue, though the roles of my seducers have switched, tag teaming.

Derek tugs my nipples between his teeth, then tenderly soothes his bite with his tongue. Patrick's mimicking Derek's treatment of my breast – though Patrick's focus is on my clit. *Nibbling and sucking.* I moan into Derek's mouth, as exhilaration rushes through my veins.

"I'm gonna come," I murmur.

"Come all over Patrick's tongue, baby. He wants to taste your sweetness," Derek urges me on. *Oh god...*

Derek ravishes one of my breasts with his mouth and massages and tugs the other with his fingers. Patrick quickly nips my clit, then spears my sex continuously with his tongue and I explode. The feeling so intense, it steals the air from my lungs and my scream is silent.

"That's my girl – Fuck you taste so good," Patrick growls.

"I want that tight, wet pussy around my cock," Derek moans, rolling to his back, then sliding up and leaning against the headboard. "Straddle my cock, baby."

I scramble to move my legs but it's like my brain has short circuited and my body is doing whatever it wants. After several failed attempts, I'm able to get up on my hands and knees and assume my requested position across Derek's hips.

"Okay baby, we're gonna try something new tonight. You're gonna take both of us. Are you ready for it?"

Oh god, oh god, oh god...

"I-I-I don't know if I can Sir."

"You're ready baby. We've been prepping your ass with plugs for a few weeks. We wouldn't attempt it if we didn't think you can handle it," Patrick idles up to my back, whispering in my ear.

"We're gonna take it slow, Sunshine," Derek reassures me. "Lift up and slide your sweet pussy down on my cock."

I did his bidding, eagerly placing the head of his cock at my entrance. Derek retakes a hold on his shaft, meticulously working the bulbous head back and forth in my slit. My eyes roll back in my head at the intoxicating feeling that erupts when he strokes it across my engorged clit. He stills, grasping my hips and pulling me down until my sex is flush with the base of his shaft. A guttural groan escapes me and he pauses for me to adjust to his size and abrupt entry.

Derek begins lifting my hips up and down. Patrick encompasses his body of around my back, reaching around to stroke my clit.

"Derek got to have your pussy first, so your ass is mine," Patrick grumbles in my ear.

The tiny quiver begins in my belly.

As if they're communicating through osmosis, Derek places his hands on my ass cheek and spreads them apart. *I feel so exposed.* A cold blob drops just above my last virginal area. I feel Patrick's finger spread the cold gooeyness between the split of my cheeks. His finger pauses at the taboo area, applying slight pressure. I immediately begin clenching Derek's cock, squeezing every inch on the withdrawal and subsequent penetrating thrusts.

Patrick inserts his finger, loosening and stretching my ass in preparation to receive his thick, massive shaft. Just his finger has me on the verge of detonation. I can't imagine having his cock buried deep within me. Patrick continues fingering my ass, while Derek slows his thrusts.

"Okay baby, I'm gonna pull out most of the way, so Patrick can ease in. I promise we're gonna take care of you. Are you ready?"

"Umm-hmmm," I stammer, trembling in my skin, nodding my head. *Fuck no, I'm not ready to have his huge dick shoved up my ass.*

"Eyes on me, baby," Derek whispers. "You have your safeword."

I feel the head of Patrick's cock at my puckered opening. I feel more cold, gooey lube and he presses in. Just a small bit, but it feels like his fist.

"FUCK, FUCK, FUCK!!!" I grit through my teeth.

"I'm gonna ignore that Sunshine. Just this once," Patrick sneers.

Derek begins massaging my clit. Patrick pulls out, waits a few seconds and pushes in again; a little farther this time.

"SHIT!" I grouse and a heated smack lands on my ass.

"Watch your mouth!"

"Watch your dick!" I snarl back, in complete self-preservation mode.

"I am. I'm gonna watch my dick bury deep in your ass."

Keeping his word, Patrick buries deep, his heavy sac resting against my sex. A sheen of moisture covers my body from the burning and stretching. Our bodies are frozen in time, allowing us to acclimate to these new sensations.

"I promise baby, once we find our rhythm, you'll be craving this from now on," Derek attempts to soothe me.

Patrick pulls out most of the way and Derek guides me by my hips down on his shaft, as he thrusts slowly upward. Derek retreats and Patrick penetrates my ass once more. The ebb and flow of our bodies continue, finding a delicious rhythm.

The nerve endings in my ass have ignited and are firing throughout my body. My pussy feels like molten lava is flowing through it. Derek is massaging my clit and Patrick is caressing my breasts. My body is over stimulated and trembling with ecstasy.

"Fuck baby – Your ass is so tight; I'm struggling to hang on."

"Your pussy is choking my cock, Sunshine. God you feel so fucking good," Derek grinds out through his clench jaw.

I hear them but I can't respond. I'm floating – soaring. I feel a pinch on my nipple and I blink several times.

"Stay with us, Sunshine. I want you in the moment, I want to hear you when you come," *Derek – beautiful Derek.*

The exhilarating rhythm continues a bit longer and Derek abruptly stills and his pulsating release sends waves of euphoric sensations through my body. He thrusts once more, gripping my clit, as Patrick roars his release – pumping, filling my ass.

The fullness of having both of them buried deep in me, marking me, controlling me, owning me – sends off shockwaves of white lights exploding behind my eyes, my sex quaking with release, as a gut-wrenching scream pierces the night.

****

A girl could get used to waking up like this; sandwiched between these two. *Pumpernickel and rye. Ha – sandwich – pumpernickel and rye. A crack myself up sometimes.*

They're both still sleeping and no way for me to get up without waking them up, so I guess I'll just keep laying here enjoying the company. I can't believe I'm still in the bed at 10AM. I never sleep this late but I've never been woken up the crack of dawn by not one raging hard on, but two. I was thankful to be able to go back sleep this morning.

My mind wanders back to last night at the club. I wonder if something's going on between Gina and Leo. They were both putting off strong vibes. I don't know much about Leo, but I assume he's around my age, considering he was Navy buddies with Isaac. There's a good bit of age difference between he and Gina. *Like I have room to talk about dating younger people. – Hypocrite.* If they do hook up, I hope he's good to Gina. She's had a pretty crappy adult life. Her former boyfriend was a Dom wannabe, abusing her in the name of BDSM. I hope *he* gets what's coming to him one day.

And Kathy, Kathy, Kathy... Bitch went and got a tattoo and didn't say a word. Not just any tattoo, oh no. A tattoo on her mound. *Yes – we will be talking.*

****

Breakfast was delicious and my belly's full. Derek and I clear the table and clean up the kitchen. Being he was the chef this morning, Patrick is relieved of KP duty and heads to the shower.

My dad always cooked breakfast on the weekends because he wanted no part of doing dishes. Of course, since he worked during the week, mom would do all the cooking and cleaning. But on the weekends, dad liked to help out some. I sure do miss him.

Gosh, I can't believe how achy and sore I am. Achy and sore in all the right places, though. I think I could actually go back to sleep. I yawn and stretch, with just a hint of knowing that lifting my arms will partially expose my butt cheeks to Derek, in temptation. Like a streak of lightning, Derek seizes the opportunity to pop my exposed ass with the dishtowel.

"Someone's being a naughty temptress. Naughty girls get popped," he chuckles.

"I like to be a naughty," I reply in a sultry tone, loosening my robe to expose my breasts to Derek.

The doorbell interrupts our sexy banter.

"I wonder who that can be," I ponder, furrowing my brow and re-tightening my robe.

"Are you expecting any one?" Derek asks nonchalantly.

"No, it's probably my neighbor, Marcy. She's probably returning my crock pot that I let her borrow the other day," I surmise, walking to the door.

I open the door expecting to see Marcy, but I'm stunned by who I see.

"Hey, Deb. Did I catch you at a bad time?"

"Scott… What are you doing here?" I fumble over my words, while using my hand to close the top of my robe up to my neck. *Crazy, I know. I was married to him, but I ain't now and he ain't seeing my goodies.* "Yeah, I'm kinda busy right now."

"Well, I thought maybe we could grab a bite to eat and continue our talk."

What?!?!

"Don't you think you should have called first? Besides, I thought that conversation *was* over."

"You don't answer or return my calls lately."

"So, you took the chance that I'd be home today."

"Pretty much. You won't return my calls. What was I supposed to do?"

"Take the hint of why I'm not calling you."

"Which is?"

Obviously, I need a bat to pound into his dense skull.

"Scott, things are awkward between us right now. Ever since the incident at mom's, after the funeral, you've been acting weird and it's freaking me out." I take a deep breath. "Scott, I think the fact that you're getting married again..."

"I'm not getting married. That's what I want to talk to you about." Scott interrupts me. "I want us to give it another try."

"Wh-What are you talking about?" My words falter. *Shit – I know Derek is nearby and can probably hear every word of this whack- a- doodle conversation.*

"Look, can I come in so we're not having this conversation in the doorway, where all your neighbors can hear?" He asks, with a touch of angst in his voice.

"I told you this is not a good time."

"God damn it, Deb. Stop being such a bitch about it and open the door!" He barks, pounding his fist on the door, trying to push it open.

"NO!" I growl, pushing back on the door.

Scott slaps his open palm on the door, countering my force to keep it open.

"I think she said no. Simple word – two letters. Yet, so misunderstood," Derek calmly remarks, stepping between me and Scott.

The color drains from Scott's face, then quickly reddens.

With a sinister laugh, Scott remarks, "Seriously, are you kidding me? What are you, his flavor of the month? Jee-zus Deb, have some respect for yourself."

"Respect? Who the hell are you to talk about respect? You lyin', cheatin' ass," I yell, trying to get around Derek, so I can knock the shit out of Scott.

Derek turns and startles me with a stern look. Clearly not happy with my dirty mouth.

"I think you should leave and let things calm down," Derek suggest to Scott.

"Look man, I don't have a problem with you." Scott attempts to cajole Derek.

"Funny, because I have one with you."

"This is between me and Deb. It has nothing to do with you and it's none of your business."

"See, that's where you're wrong. Anything to do with Debra *is* my business. You would do well to remember that." Derek's advice laced with warning.

Oh shit – I've never seen that look on Derek's face.

"Man, I know your type. You need a lonely woman so she can stroke your ego. You fuck'em then leave'm."

Derek pauses a moment, the wheels spinning in his head. He takes a deep breath before continuing. *I see fury simmering just below the surface.*

"What the fuck is your problem, Scott? Just leave," I shriek in frustration.

Derek slams me with a fierce look. A definite warning to shut my mouth.

"You need to go – Now!" Derek growls.

"What's all the yelling about?" Patrick asks, stepping up behind Derek, wearing shorts and a towel around his neck. *Jeez – he's sexy as hell.*

"What the fuck, Deb? You having some kind of orgy up in here," Scott howls.

"D – who the hell is this?" Patrick asks Derek with a shrug.

"He's the ex."

God, why can't the floor just open up and swallow me whole.

"God damn, Deb, fucking two at a time. Are you a fucking whore?"

Patrick lunges forward and all I hear is the sickening crack of broken bones. "Who the fuck are you talking to, you little shit?" Patrick roars, grabbing Scott by his shirt. Blood pouring from Scott's nose.

"Oh my god," I gasp, not believing what I'm seeing before me.

"Don't ever speak to her or about her with that filthy tone again. Your punk ass better show her all the respect she deserves. Got it!" Patrick drills, slapping Scott in the chest.

"I'm calling the cops," Scott threatens.

"Too late, I'm already here," Patrick snarls back.

"I'm gonna sue!"

"Let's talk. I'm his attorney," Derek adds with a snicker.

"Time to go, prick," Patrick taunts, shoving Scott down the corridor.

CHAPTER 15

What a restless night! I soooo need the solace of this drive down to mom's. The stress of yesterday's melee was more than I can handle. I tossed and turned all night, even after coming multiple times from Sirs' delicious, sexual torture.

I replay the events over and over in my head. What is Scott thinking? He's suddenly not getting married and he thinks I'm willing to give *us* another try. *Is he insane?* Then acts like a total Neanderthal when he doesn't get his away. *Yeah, that really makes me want to get back together. Idiot...*

I'm quite impressed with how calm Derek stayed, even with Scott provoking him. Being an attorney, I guess he's used to that.

Jee-zus, I never expected Patrick to punch him. He didn't think twice. When he'd heard enough – BAM!

I hope Scott calms down and doesn't do anything stupid. I don't want Derek or Patrick to have any repercussions from reacting to Scott's asinine behavior.

****

"Mom, the place looks great. Isaac's crew did a fabulous job on the sunroom," admiring her plants and decorations.

"It's truly a blessing, all the work they did on the house. Did you ever get the bill settled with Isaac? I never received a statement."

"Yeah, it's all taken care of. *Which isn't a lie. Isaac took care of all of it. He wouldn't accept a dime.*

"Debra, I have the money to pay for it. Let me pay you back."

"Mom, everything is good. Save that money for a rainy day. Or, better yet, take a trip with Aunt Gladys. *No way in hell I'm telling her Isaac did all the work for free. She would feel indebted to him and she would fret too much over it. Better that she never knows the truth.*

"You two should take a cruise," I suggest.

"Oh, by the way, I received an invitation to the wedding. I'm so happy for Katherine. She is deserving of some happiness in her life."

"Yes, she is. I think she found her a good one this time."

"Well… Did I understand the invitation correctly? The wedding is a *surprise*?" Mom asks mystified.

"It's a surprise for Kathy. Isaac is planning everything. She only had to pick out her dress, which she did this past week. She has no idea where the wedding is taking place. I think I would be crazy not knowing," I concede.

"Oh my, I think I would be a nervous wreck. However, I can't wait to see how it turns out," Mom says excitedly.

"Neither can I." The conversation pauses and we let the excitement of the nuptials settle in.

"Well, how are things with you, sweetie? Are you seeing anyone special?"

Oh hell, what am I going to say? She caught me completely off guard. My mind's still reeling from Scott's antics yesterday. I hadn't even considered the fact that mom would question me about dating. I decide to buy me a smidgen of time by playing dumb.

"I'm sorry, Mom. I was daydreaming about the wedding. What'd you say?"

"Oh, sorry dear. Just wondering if you're seeing anyone."

"Uh…"

"I just want you to find happiness, too," she continues her thought, while I sit speechless.

Yeah, I've met someone - two someones, and I'm very happy at the moment. But I can't tell her about Derek and Patrick. She would never understand. She would be so hurt and disappointed in me. It would devastate her to know what I'm doing, how I'm living my life. I can't hurt her like that, so soon after Dad's death.

"No, I'm not seeing any one," I carefully try to hide the deceit in my voice.

My god, I just lied right to Mom's face. What does that say about me? About my relationship with Derek and Patrick? They warned me of the ramifications of this type of relationship, considered by most, to be perverse.

I take Mom to lunch at her favorite restaurant. The food is always wonderful, but my tummy is queasy and I've lost my appetite. Guilt is weighing me down, from lying to my mom and not having the courage to acknowledge my relationship with the guys.

****

Music is normally my companion on the two-hour drive back home, but today I drive in silence. Silence, apart from the voices of reason, my conscience, and my heart. They're all at war with each other. It's time to take an honest look at my life.

The most obvious point, is the differences in our age. I'm eight years older than both of them. It really wouldn't be much of an issue, except for the fact I'm 46 years old and past my baby making years. *Not that I'm certain the relationship would develop to that stage, but I have to consider the possibility.* They are younger and probably want a family one day, and I can't give them that. Besides, that's a whole new set of obstacles that I can't wrap my brain around right now. *A ménage with a baby, um, no.*

And again, I'm eight years older and they're smoldering hot. Men only get better with age. Women fight gravity and gravity always wins. Everything will start drooping and sagging. They don't want to be stuck with an old woman.

Even if we can work all of that out and get past it, ultimately it comes down to the fact that it's morally wrong and goes against what I was taught - A girl grows up, falls in love with the man of her dreams, not the men of her dreams.

I didn't have the courage to tell my own mother about my relationship with Derek and Patrick, how in the world could I tell anyone else, expect them to accept it.

The past several weeks have been absolutely amazing. If I could live in a bubble with the both of them, shutting the world out... I would. Unfortunately, I can't shut out the world, so it's time to face reality.

I've had several missed calls from both Derek and Patrick. I don't want to talk to either of them right now. I shoot them both a text explaining I'm exhausted from the trip and I'm heading to bed, but I want to meet them in town for dinner tomorrow night.

****

Another sleepless night. My mind is racing and my heart is heavy and torn. Everything I touched at work today became a mess. It was an all-out shitty day and the night doesn't look any better.

Apprehension builds, while I wait for Derek and Patrick to join me for dinner, as always they're right on time.

Hugs and kisses exchange and my resolve waivers. *God, I love being with them.*

"I need to talk to you both about some things on my mind."

"Of course, baby. What's going on?" Derek asks, concern showing on his face, mimicking the look on Patrick's.

"I can see something's troubling you. Let's talk," Patrick urges.

I take a deep breath and begin to ramble with all my thoughts and concerns about them, me, us.

Unbelievably, neither have spoken nor tried to interrupt.

"I just need some time to work this out in my head, think things through. Unfortunately, my mind turns to mush whenever I'm around the two of you and I can't think rationally. So, I think it's best for me, for us, to take a b-break." I'm fighting back tears, trying not to break down.

Moments pass and neither have responded to anything I've said. I nearly crumble under their scrutinizing gaze, that's penetrating my soul.

"I'm not going to try and negate your concerns. You have mentioned a couple of issues that would definitely warrant soul searching conversations, if our relationship progressed to a more permanent arrangement. With that being said, some of your concerns are unfounded, based on lack of confidence and the perceptions of others," Patrick declares.

"However, we're not going to push you, Debra. We'll give you the time you need. We will not inundate you with pressure. Though this is not what we want, we respect you and your need for space," Derek attests with great sincerity.

I'm trembling in my struggle to remain composed.

"We just ask that the lines of communication remain open."

"Agreed," I murmur.

****

Derek & Patrick

"I knew that shit with her ex on Saturday, affected her more than she was letting on," Patrick declares.

"You knew this wouldn't be easy, Pat. Not only is she inexperienced in ménage, she's a novice in the lifestyle. Hell, this is new for us; trying to establish a relationship among the three of us. I think the combination of the melee on Saturday, coupled with visiting her mom, was a bit overwhelming. She's still testing the waters; unsure if this is the lifestyle she really wants. She's torn between her desires and her morals."

"You're right, D. We just need to give her some space. You know what they say – 'if you love something, set it free, and it can come back'. Something like that..."

"Love? What are you saying, Pat?" Derek shakes his head in dismay, at the words coming from the self-professed 'confirmed bachelor'.

****

"Girl, what in the hell is going on?" Kathy's question is laced with worry, as she slides into the bench seat.

"Hey to you, too," I pop off.

"*Hey*... You look like shit," she admonishes.

"Gee, thanks. I feel like shit. I haven't slept in three days."

"Oh sweetie, why didn't you call me? The only thing I know is what Derek and Patrick said to Isaac and then he relayed to me. So... I know nothing."

I continue twirling the wrapper from my straw into knots, trying to figure out where to start, unable to look her in the eyes.

"Does is have something to do with the stunt Scott pulled on Saturday? You seemed okay Saturday night when we talked."

"No, it's nothing to do with him. It's just... Time to face reality and stop living a dream."

"I'm not following," Kathy rubs her temples. "You've been the happiest I've seen you in a very long time. Who got in your head?"

"Me... I got my head out of my ass and started thinking about real life, not a fantasy," I bury my face in my hands. "I went to visit mom Sunday. She asked me if I was seeing anyone. I panicked and couldn't bring myself to say anything about Derek and Patrick."

"Of course you couldn't tell your mom. It's still too early. You're trying to figure out what's going on yourself."

"Well, that led me to think about our age difference, kids, marriage, and the chances of this relationship working in the long run," I stop and ponder my own words.

"It's not that I would never tell Mom. If we were building a long-term relationship, I would risk my relationship and tell her. But why tell her, something I know would hurt her, when I don't know where my relationship with Derek and Patrick is heading. It's not like I would engage in another threesome. I most definitely would not.

The Sun and the Moon and the Stars aligned with my Sirs – I mean Patrick and Derek. That won't happen again.

Regardless, Mom was only part of it. I'm sure they will eventually want a family and that ship has sailed for me. And come on Kathy, they're unbelievably sexy. It's only a matter of time before the newness wears off and they move on to a younger, more voluptuous companion."

"Have you talked to them about their desires to have children? To find a younger version?"

"No, of course not," I reluctantly admit.

"So, you just made those decisions for them," she says with an insolent tone.

"It's what's best…"

"Yeah, I can see that. Dark circles do wonders for you," She snarks.

"Look, enough of this. We have more important things to talk about. Like a bachelorette party," I squeal, needing a change in the conversation. "That's what this lunch meeting is for."

CHAPTER 16

This limo is super stretch. There's seven cackling women in here already and I swear seven to ten more can easily fit. Neon lights around the floor, as well as every button, lever, and compartment.

Isaac's only request/demand related to the bachelorette party, was for us to take a limo instead of carpooling. He arranged for us to be picked up and dropped off at home, so we wouldn't be tempted to drive. Marcy and I will be dropped off last, since we live in the same building and there's safety in numbers.

We just picked up Jean. All the ladies are here: Katherine, Marcy, Gina, Alexandria, Jean, Charlotte, and me. Time to get this party started.

After a loud and rather raucous dinner, we head and over to Cowboys, where the real fun we'll begin.

Our table awaits us. I reserved the table and came by earlier this afternoon to decorate it. Thankfully, no one has bothered it and it looks very festive. A hot pink and purple penis centerpiece made from balloons, draws howling laughter from everyone. Penis shaped confetti is scattered across the table.

Within a few minutes, all the ladies have their blinking buttons on, warning of their proclivities; Tease, Bad girl, Wild, Sexy, Flirt, Virgin-ish, and of course, Bride. Cock-shaped suckers dangle from hot pink beaded necklaces around our necks, as well as adorn the tip of our straws.

Kathy and I saw a band last year at a music festival that we really, really liked. I signed up for their email alerts and received one saying they would be playing at Cowboys this weekend. I had planned to ask her about coming to see them. When she and Isaac decided to get married this month, I thought it would be perfect for her bachelorette party.

McKenzies Mill takes the stage and kicks off the night with 'Dirty Things', Kathy's favorite song of theirs.

The club is rocking and electricity is sparking in the air. We're movin' and groovin' to every song; feathers floating in the air from our boas. The band's playing their hard driving country originals, as well as their version of some of the best rock and country classics and today's hits.

There's over a 25-year span in age among our group, but you could never tell. We're all having a fabulous time. It's actually been great opportunity to get to know Gina, Alexandria, and Charlotte, a little better. I wasn't exactly sure how this was all going to work out. Charlotte's a Domme; Kathy, Gina, Alexandria, and myself are subs (*well I was... not sure what I am now*), and then Marcy and Jean have no connection to the lifestyle.

As expected, a few topics of conversation have caused Jean and Marcy's cheeks to run crimson. However, after a few Vegas Bombs and a Buttery Nipple, they're trash talking with the rest of us.

I'm thankful the conversations have not drifted to my trio fiasco. Cutting loose is just what I needed tonight. We've had a few men approach, wanting to dance, but for the most part, we've been left to our liquid vices; shaken our asses like nobody's watching.

Even with all her Bride accessories, one idiot approached Kathy to dance. I advised him, if he wanted to keep his balls attached, he needed to step away. I warned him Isaac would shove his balls down his throat, after he broke his jaw. I giggled when the color left his face.

Other than watching Charlotte, all of five feet tall, put a towering prick in his place; (*she needs to teach a class in self-confidence and classy smack talk*) the highlight of the night is watching McKenzies Mill perform their version of '*Get Off on the Pain*'. The lead singer stepping off stage, sharing the mic with Kathy, as she wails out the chorus. So happy I'm still sober enough to record this on my phone.

****

The Bachelor Party

Isaac has a penchant for bourbon so we decide to have a bourbon tasting for his bachelor party, along with the little poker.

Each of the guys - Zeke, Tiny, Leo, Edward, Katherine's sons – Ben and Matt, Derek and myself – have contributed a bottle of bourbon to sample. Everyone but Matt, that is. He's Katherine's youngest. Not 21, so he won't be partaking in the sampling, but Isaac wanted them both included in the festivities.

Noah's Mill, Buffalo Trace, Pappy's, Hudson's, Woodford Reserve, Blanton's, and Jefferson's are all on the sampling block.

I was a little surprised Isaac agreed to close the club for the night. But being the women are out partying with Katherine, it made sense to have his bachelor party the same night.

I hope Sunshine is having a good time. Not too good, but an OK time. I really think Derek and I should be waiting on her when she gets home. No... we're giving her space.

A couple of hands of poker and a few rounds of bourbon, everyone seems to be having a good time, especially Matt. He's won a hundred bucks playing poker. Guess there might be a connection with being sober and winning poker.

"Bourbon and poker. The only thing missing is good pussy," Leo proclaims.

"Oh...we got pussy here," Isaac's spouts off.

The rumbling around the room calms, and we all look at Isaac, trying to decipher his statement.

"Where you got them hid, man?" Leo chuckles.

"They're not hidden. They're sitting right there," Isaac nods toward me and Derek.

"What the hell you talking about, Ike?" Derek grumbles.

"You two are being pussies. You're letting your sub control you."

"Ike, it's not like that. Man, you don't understand," I bark back.

"I understand your sub is new to this lifestyle and having normal insecurities. Her problem is, she has pussy Doms allowing her to flounder around in doubt, instead of providing her with firm guidance."

"Our situation is different. The stigma of being involved in a ménage is huge," Derek argues.

"You think there's not a stigma to spanking your partner, handcuffing your wife, or caning your husband? Derek, there's a stigma to every part of life, whether it involves BDSM or not. You can always find somebody who has something negative to say about what you're doing in your life. What you have to do is decide not to give a fuck about what other people think, and live your life – your way."

You could hear a pin drop in this place. The look on Ben's face is priceless.

"Point taken," Derek sighs, hanging his head.

I'm trying to piece together my ass that Isaac just ripped into.

"Now, line up the Pappy's. There's too much whiskey in those bottles. Drink up," Isaac orders, slapping me on the back, a gesture I'm still in his good graces.

****

"Who the hell is ringing my phone this early in the morning?"

My head is pounding. Kathy and her damn tequila. I don't know how that girl can drink that shit and be unaffected by it. *Well, she may have been a little affected, since the last thing I saw was her ass being tossed over Isaac's shoulder.*

I reach over, and pick up my phone, and see its Mom calling.

"Hey Mom," I answer groggily, yawning into the phone.

"Debra Leònne, what on earth are you doing? Is it true? How could you do this?" She sobs into the phone.

"Mom! Calm down. What are you talking about? Why are you so upset?" Shuddering sobs are all I can hear. "Mom, please calm down. Take a deep breath and tell me what has you so upset."

"Are – are you involved in deviant behavior, Debra? Sexual orgies? Oh my god, I can't believe I'm having to ask you this."

"Mom, what are you talking about?"

"Scott, Scott called me and said he was concerned about you. That you're involved in some kind of sex cult," her words broken up by sobs.

"A sex cult?!?! No, Mom. I'm not in a sex cult. When did Scott call you?"

"Last night. Debra, I'm worried sick about you," her ebbing sobs increase again.

"Mom, please calm down. Listen, I'm gonna shower and I'll be down as soon as I can."

Ire is flowing through me like a wildfire out of control. *Who the fuck does he think he is? He's a raving lunatic.*

I debate for a moment whether to call him now or wait until I'm on the road. Mom is in full blown melt down, so I decide to wait and call him from the car. I want to get to mom as soon as possible.

"Deb? I'm surprised -"

"Who the fuck do you think you are?!?! How dare you call my mother and spew vile lies about me! Do you have any fucking clue how upset she is? My god, Scott, you could have caused her to have a stroke. What is wrong with you? Sex cult? Really... You fucking idiot."

"I'm concerned about you, Deb. Your recent behavior is alarming."

"Alarming, you don't even know what you're talking about."

"I know what I saw."

"And what *did* you see? *NOTHING!!!* You didn't see a damn thing. Besides, I don't give a fuck if you saw me fucking five men and three women, it's none of your fucking business. And you definitely had no right upsetting Mom like this. You better hope and pray nothing happens to her."

My hands are shaking with rage. I need to calm down before I wreck.

"Deb, I never meant to upset your mom. I just –"

"Shut up – just shut up. I don't want to hear anymore. I'm telling you now – do not call her again. For that matter, don't call me."

I end the call and slam my phone on the passenger seat, growling out my frustration.

****

I knock on the door first, then use my key let myself in. I find mom sitting at the dining room table with her head in her hands.

"Mom, are you okay?"

The look on her face breaks my heart. The hurt and worry in her swollen eyes. *I could choke Scott right now.* I lean over, wrapping my arms and body over and around her.

"I don't know what Scott was thinking, calling and upsetting you like this."

"Where did he get that idea from? Why would he say those things about you?"

Telling mom about my relationship with Derek and Patrick is the dilemma that pushed me to take a break from the relationship and think things through. I didn't want to hurt her. However, Scott stole that choice for me with his spiteful phone call to her. He's left me no alternative, but to tell her about Derek and Patrick.

A river of tears flow during my confession, of sorts. Though not as horrid as Scott made it to be, I clearly see the hurt in Mom's eyes.

A persistent lull in the conversation the silence, allowing Mom to gather her thoughts. The lingering silence that terrified me as a child, because I knew I had disappointed my parents and now waited for their judgement. I remember Derek saying that waiting is its own form of bondage. No shackles or cuffs, nor rope or chain, can bind one more tightly than time.

Finally, Mom breaks her silence, "Debra, you know we weren't staunch churchgoers, but your father and I tried to instill in you, moral values and the knowledge of right and wrong. It crushed us when you divorced Scott. We believed strongly in the sanctity of marriage – *'til death do us part'*. But I also believe in you. I know you had exhausted all means to salvage your marriage, if divorce was your only option. I don't know everything, but I know Scott hurt you and broke your trust."

"He did, many times over," I confess for the first time.

"I grew up believing in the marriage of one man and one woman. I also put credence in what others thought of me. But life continued to teach me and open my mind. I realized the thoughts of others didn't provide my happiness. I was putting more value in someone else's thoughts and beliefs than my own. One day, I began interpreting things for myself, instead of listening to someone tell me how it should be. My mind opened even more. Your father and I shared our open-mindedness," Mom's eyes sparkle, as she takes my hands in hers and continues.

"Debra, everyone has a right to love whomever they choose. Who has the right to tell someone their love is wrong? I still believe in marriage; the joining of those in love and committed to each other, regardless of their gender.

So if I believe that, how can I not believe that love can be shared by more than two in a relationship? It may not work for me, but that doesn't mean it won't work for someone else.

If I can give you one last piece of advice – find *your* happiness. Don't let your happiness be determined by the opinions of others."

Now, I'm the one sobbing profusely. All this time, I've been so worried about hurting her, that I didn't give her a chance to voice her opinion. I'd decided it for her, making assumptions. I assumed her beliefs were the same as she'd taught me as a child. I never considered her feelings had evolved. Guess I should spend more time talking *with* Mom and not at her.

"Do you love them?" She asks, clutching my hand within hers.

"I – don't know... yes. Yes, I love them. But it takes more than love, Mom. There are many things to consider; our age difference, children..."

"Those are things to discuss with them. You can't assume how they feel. You have to communicate."

CHAPTER 17

I let Patrick and Derek know that I needed a few days to think, and I would be in touch soon. I disconnected myself from the world and did a lot of soul searching the past couple of days. I spent my time thinking a lot about what Mom said.

I'm thrilled she is open to the prospect of me having a relationship with Derek and Patrick, but I still have questions and insecurities. However, Mom and Kathy are right. I can't make presumptions about their desire for children or finding someone closer to their age. I must talk it over with them in order to eradicate my hesitancy to pursue this relationship.

I check my phone and notice I have eight missed phone calls. *That's odd. Eight missed calls since lunch.* I check the phone log and see five missed calls from Patrick and three from Kathy.

Knowing a call to Patrick maybe lengthy, I decide to give Kathy a quick call first.

"Deb – Thank God. Have you talked to Patrick? Kathy answers hastily.

"No, not yet. What's wrong? You're scaring me," my heart jolts.

"It's Derek. Shortly after lunch, he collapsed in court, clutching his chest. He was rushed to the hospital."

I hear her words but they're not registering in my brain. Derek – chest – hospital.

"Oh My God! What? Where is he?"

"He's at Northside. Patrick heard the call over the radio and he met the ambulance at the hospital. I'm on my way. Isaac's heading back from Augusta."

"I'm on my way. I'm leaving now."

I end the call, notify my manager and fly out the door. *My god, he's too young to have a heart attack. He's never mentioned heart problems, high blood pressure, nothing.*

I run into the ER, huffing and puffing. "Derek Moore... Could you tell me where he is? He was brought in by ambulance."

The woman taps into the computer. A little too lackadaisical to me.

"Are you family?" The placid woman asks.

"Uh, I'm...uh,"

"I'm only allowed to release information to family."

"I'm, uh – his girlfriend," I bend the truth.

"I'm sorry, ma'am, family only," the unemotional woman responds, clearly not sorry.

"Look, you don't understand. He doesn't have family here. His grandmother is his nearest relative and she lives in Tennessee." I explain. "Please, I need to know how he is. Have some compassion."

She taps on the computer again. "I can tell you he's in surgery, but that's all I can say. Surgery waiting area is on the second floor."

The elevator doors open onto the second floor. I frantically look for directions to the waiting area.

"Deb..."

I turn toward *his* voice – *Patrick*. Nothing else crosses my mind, but getting to him as fast as I can. He wraps me up in his arms and the tears I've been struggling to hold back, burst through and streak down my face.

"Wh-what happened to him? Is he going to be okay? Did he have a heart attack?" I rant hysterically.

"Ssshhh, baby. Calm down. It's not his heart."

"It's not??? OH THANK GOD!!! What's wrong? Why's he in surgery?"

"It's his gallbladder. He's going to be fine."

"His gallbladder???"

"Yeah. He has several stones. Apparently, sometimes a gallbladder attack can feel like a heart attack. I have a feeling all the bourbon Saturday night didn't help the situation."

"How did you find out anything? The witch downstairs was no help, other than sending me up here."

"I have connections," he chuckles into the top of my head.

"Oh Sir, I've missed you so much," I nuzzle into his chest. Then a tinge of pain strikes and I push away from his chest. "I can call you Sir, can't I? Please tell me I can. I know we have lots to talk about, but this feels so good, being here in your arms. The only thing missing is my other Sir." I squeeze him a little tighter.

"I am your Master, along with Derek. You belong to us, Sunshine. Yes, we do have a lot to talk about, when Derek is back on his feet," he holds my gaze before kissing my lips so tender.

We turn the corner and walk into the waiting room to join Kathy. I know this procedure is considered routine, but I can't relax until I know he's in recovery.

After 45 minutes of pacing across the floor, the doctor enters the waiting area.

"Mike, how is he?" Patrick greets the doctor, obviously knowing him.

"The surgery went just as planned and Derek's doing great."

"When will he be able to go home?" I interrupt.

"Oh ... Debra, this is Mike Ying. Sorry, Dr. Mike Ying," Patrick chides.

"You can call me Mike."

"Nice to meet you," I reply, shaking his hand.

"I'm going to keep Derek overnight, since it's late in the day. He'll be able to go first thing in the morning."

"When can we see him?" I ask.

"Give them a half hour or so and they'll let you back to see him briefly. Then he'll be transferred to a regular room for the night and you'll be able to visit longer."

"Thanks Mike."

"Yes, thank you for all your help." I reiterate Patrick's sentiment.

Relief floods me and I realize just how empty my life would be if Derek or Patrick weren't in it. The momentary thought that I could possibly lose Derek forever paralyzes me. Thoughts run rampant through my mind. Patrick has a dangerous job, putting his life on the line every day. I could lose either of them in a blink of an eye. No one knows what tomorrow will bring. We must live each day as if it were our last. With no regrets...

Patrick and I go back to recovery and Derek's still very groggy. A smile emerges on his face. I'm hoping it's because he recognizes us. His words or should I say grumbles, are incoherent, so it's difficult to communicate with him. I let him know we can only stay a moment, but we'll see him when they get him settled in a room.

"Come here, Sunshine."

It's amazing how much more alert Derek is in an hour's time. I walk over to his bedside. He reaches up and tangles his hand in my hair, pulling my face down close to his.

"It's over, Sunshine," he whispers in my ear.

My heart begins fluttering. *What does he mean – it's over? Did he change his mind about having a relationship? Did he get tired of waiting? Did Scott get to him?* The thoughts bouncing around in my head cause panic to set in.

"Sir..."

"It's over – your running, your thinking – it's over. I'm not allowing you to shut us out," he winces in pain.

"Ssshh, just rest. When you're better, we'll talk." I try keeping him calm.

"You belong to us. Discussion over."

I'm not going to argue with him, because he's right, though we do have things to talk through.

"I'm picking you up in the morning and taking you to my place."

"You have to work. I can get a ride or call a cab."

"ABSOLUTELY NOT! I know I'm new to this lifestyle and have a lot to learn, but I do know that Masters and Mistresses, Dominants and Dommes, and Sirs and Madames take care of their subs. I also know that's a two-way street. Subs take care of their Masters, too. And I'm taking care of you. End of discussion," I use his play on words.

Derek gives me a sinister look with an arched brow. I heed his warning look.

"End of discussion, *Sir*"

I hear snickering behind me, but I'm not sure if it came from Patrick or Kathy. I know it wasn't Isaac. *For some reason, I don't think he's the snickering type.*

****

Derek's had a good day and feels up to eating a regular meal. I make chicken and dumplings and have them ready when Patrick gets *home*. I warn Derek of the potential problems of overeating so soon after surgery. My warning falls on deaf ears as he finishes his second bowl and Patrick inhales his third.

Patrick and I migrate to my bed, where Derek's resting, find a spot and lay across the bed.

"Kids – do you want them?" Patrick spurts out to no one in particular.

"I grew up thinking I did, but I honestly I haven't given much thought about it in the last few, or more like five years, Derek responds.

"Did you and your ex want kids?" Patrick presses the issue.

"Early in our marriage, we tried. Of course, we weren't successful. We both went to the doctor and nothing conclusive was determined to prevent a pregnancy. At the time, we didn't have the thousands of dollars to invest in In Vitro or other alternative measures. We decided to leave it to nature. I became pregnant once, but had a miscarriage early on. I figured we weren't meant to have children. Hindsight, it was for the best. I would never want to drag children through the mess my marriage disintegrated to."

"How about you?" I nod my question to Patrick.

"I think I eventually want kids. But like Derek said, I haven't really thought about it in a long time."

"But let me clear up something – us wanting a relationship with you is not dependent on the ability to procreate. We don't live in the 1800s, when people had a dozen kids to work the farm. Lots of people never have kids. Some people use In Vitro, plus there's plenty of children in the world that need a home," Derek clarifies their stance on the issue.

"Now, we're well aware that you were in the second grade when we were born. I'll admit our age difference may have been an issue back then, but I don't believe there are any laws preventing it now. We are consenting adults," Patrick laughs out loud.

"Pat, I think she feels we'll eventually trade her in on a *'younger model'*," Derek mocks, as if I'm not sitting here.

"Huh, I see. I guess we'll have to come up with a way to convince her of our commitment to her," Patrick continues talking over me.

"Don't patronize me. My concerns are valid and reasonable," I huff, feigning hurt feelings.

"Oh, your concerns have been duly noted and addressed. Do you have anything to add, D?"

"The only current concern I see that we have, is determining a permanent residence, being we all have separate homes," Derek adds. "But it's not an urgent matter."

****

Two days cooped up inside, Derek is pacing like a caged tiger. The three of us decide to hit the local diner for breakfast.

Bellies full, we climb back in Patrick's truck. Thankfully, it's a four door super cab, super something. It has four doors and that's all that matters to me.

We turn right out of the parking lot instead of turning left to head back to my place.

"Where are we heading?" I ask, leaning up between the front seats.

"We have a stop to make before heading home," Patrick answers.

I sit back, enjoying the ride. It feels weird sitting up so high, riding down the road. My Camry doesn't sit low to the ground, but it certainly is much lower than this truck.

We slow down and bump across the entrance to the parking lot of a small strip mall. There are several different types of businesses here, so I have no clue where we're going. Patrick weaves through the lot, narrowing the prospects. He finds a spot, parks, and we disembark our elevated transportation. Realization of our destination quickly dawns.

"What are we doing here?" I ask perplexed.

"What do you think you do at a tattoo shop?" Derek sarcastically replies.

"Who's getting a tattoo?" Perplexity continuing in my voice.

"We are," Patrick says, motioning toward Derek.

"Oh..."

The guys engage in a conversation with a huge, burly man behind the counter. I'm mesmerized by all the tattoo designs hanging on the wall, but I try to focus on what's transpiring between Sirs and the human bear behind the counter. Patrick takes out a piece of paper and I catch a glimpse of a drawing.

"You both want this design?" The man asks.

"Yeah – on my upper left arm." Patrick confirms.

"And my upper right." Derek completes the confirmation.

"Whoa – wait. What are y'all doing?" I spout off. "Is that a sun?"

"It is. A tribal design," Patrick says.

"What does it say below the sun?"

"Soleil," Derek adds.

"Soleil?"

"It's French for sun or sunshine."

"Ooooh..." I respond raising my eyebrows in surprise. You're getting them for me?" I shriek.

"We are," Patrick admits.

"We want to alleviate any doubt you have about our commitment to you and this relationship," Derek expands on Patrick's few words.

"A tattoo is permanent. Don't you think it's a little soon to be making such grand gestures?"

"We're confident in our feelings for you." Patrick declares. "So the answer to your question is, no."

I can't believe what they're doing. This is a bold step. This commitment can't be one, I mean... two sided. It has to be all or nothing.

"Well, if y'all are getting one, I want one, too," I insist, shocked as the words tumble out of my mouth. I've never wanted a tattoo. Now, here I am almost demanding one.

"What are you going to get?" Patrick inquires suspiciously.

"I don't know. I'm thinking."

"Maybe you should wait until you know for sure," Derek suggests. "Like you said, it is permanent."

I ponder a bit, looking at their design. I glance up and notice a tattoo of a wolf howling at the moon, and *wah-la* – I got it.

I explain my idea to Patrick and Derek. Patrick doodles a little more and shares the altered design with the big, burly guy.

Four and a half hours later, we all walk out, each having a tattoo representing us. Derek and Patrick have the original tribal Sun with a crescent Moon and a cluster of twinkling stars in the center, with 'Soleil' scripted below.

I have a slightly more feminine version of the Sun, along with the Moon and stars in the middle. Below, I have the script letters D and P arranged in the shape of a heart. The beautiful design is located on my upper back between my shoulders. I absolutely love it. The Sun and the Moon and the Stars aligned...

****

At Mom's insistence, as well as Sirs, we drove down to Mom's for Sunday dinner. Since our talk, mom has been chomping at the bit to meet the guys. They also, have insisted on having the opportunity to set things right with Mom and settle her mind.

A modern day twist on *'Guess Who's Coming to Dinner'* times two. Mom fixed her delicious fried chicken, that I still haven't been able to get right, creamed potatoes, collard greens, Mac and cheese, and homemade biscuits. We all indulge to gluttonous capacity. Being only five days post-op, I'm sure Derek will pay for this meal later.

"Mrs. Giroux, thank you for having Derek and I for dinner today."

"Please, call me Mary. And it was my pleasure."

"Yes, thank you," Derek adds his own gratitude.

"I know the discovery of our relationship has been difficult and unsettling for you. Patrick and I want you to know that we have the utmost respect for Debra and care for her very much. In all honesty Mrs. Giroux, we love her, both together and in our separate ways."

Oh my, I think I know how a fly on the wall feels. Just sitting and observing the surroundings.

"Derek's right. Though our relationship may be salacious in the opinions of others, I promise you that our feelings for Debra are honorable and loving."

Oh my goodness – if they keep this kind of talk up, my head will explode, as well as my heart.

"What I want most for my daughter, is to be happy. I can see you both give this to her. I know her father would feel the same way."

I hate the fact that Mom was blindsided by Scott's phone call, but it did force me to face the truth and deal with it. In doing so, I've never been happier.

CHAPTER 18

The fullness is overwhelming. I feel so dominated wedged between their bodies; my legs wrapped around Patrick's waist, his cock buried deep in my sex. At the same time, my ass is completely exposed. Derek slowly forging into my newly discovered area of pleasure. Tight, forbidden, taboo –

Derek is seated deep and Patrick begins his slow withdrawal. The painstakingly slow movement ignites each and every nerve in my core. As Patrick breaches my sex once again, Derek retreats slowly and very deliberately, dousing the fire within me with gasoline. An inferno erupts as their rhythm sets; sending me into an erotic fervor.

My legs remain around Patrick's waist, while my upper body languishes back against Derek's chest. I thought sex standing up was a figment of my imagination, a dream. My Masters, my Sirs... Make dreams come true.

"Who do you belong to, Debra?" Patrick grips my chin, demanding my attention.

"You – I belong to my Sirs."

"You like having your pussy and your ass filled with cock?" Derek growls, biting my shoulder.

"God – YES!!! I love how my Masters fuck me."

Their thrusts continue, alternating and increasing with intensity. I grip Patrick shoulders to keep my balance. Patrick leans slightly back, placing his shoulders flush to the wall, while his hips pulsate feverishly into, ricocheting my ass off Derek's cock.

"Master, please, I'm so close…"

"Not yet, Sunshine."

"Grrrr…" I'm trying so hard but I just can't hold out much longer.

"Growling will only get you denied, Sunshine." Patrick mumbles, as his thrusts slow and Derek's stop.

"No, no, no – please." I beg.

"Please? Please what?" Patrick demands.

"Please don't stop, Sir. It feels soooo good."

Patrick tweaks my nipple, pulling and elongating it to a

stiffened peak. His thrusts pick up momentum as Derek drives in an alternating rhythm.

On the precipice of ecstasy, Derek reaches around and pinches my clit, sending me over the edge. As a plummet into a titillating abyss, Derek and Patrick each roar their release.

****

With no time for cuddling, it's a revolving door on the shower. Derek and Patrick are heading over to Isaac's, to meet the guys. Kathy and the girls are coming here for a night of wine and relaxation before the big day tomorrow.

"It's gonna be weird sleeping at my place tonight," Patrick professes, kissing the top of my head, tweaking my nipple before he steps away.

"Yeah, I've gotten used to snuggling up to this ass," Derek agrees, smacking my exposed ass cheek. "I do, however, think we should get a king size bed for Christmas."

"I'll be sure to let Santa know," I tease.

"So what's the plan for you ladies tonight?" Patrick inquires.

"Just a quiet night here tonight. Some wine and just chillin'. Kathy's staying here tonight. The others will meet us in the morning to get our hair and nails done."

"Then you're driving Kathy to the wedding," Derek's statement is more like a question.

"Yes. We're getting dressed there, so we'll be there by two."

****

Hair and nails done, Kathy and I run over to her house to drop food off for their new puppy, Django. Ben and Matt are watching the dogs, Max and new puppy Django, at her old house, while Kathy and Isaac go on their honeymoon.

"Thanks for running me by the house. They only sell the puppy food in small bags and I want to make sure Django has enough. Max has plenty."

"No problem. Besides, I love cuddling this sweet fur baby," I nuzzle my nose against his wet one. "Has Isaac told you where you're going on your honeymoon?"

"Nope."

"How are you supposed to pack?"

"He said I wouldn't be wearing anything."

"Mmmm... Yep, sounds like him," I laugh out loud.

"He did finally relent and told me to pack a few things for warmer weather. He can be impossible sometimes."

"Well, I hope you're getting used to it, 'cause you'll be

marrying him in a few hours. Speaking of – we need to be going. We have a bit of a ride," I chuckle, thinking of how Kathy must feel, being completely unaware of her own wedding.

After an hour-long drive, mostly done in silence, we arrive at a simply marked, inconspicuous driveway. Kathy soaked up the scenery along the way trying to decipher the destination. I precede down the driveway and feel like I've traveled across the country to the beautiful Southwest.

A breathtaking collection of white stone, adobe styled buildings come into view. Buildings seemingly plucked from the deserts of New Mexico and indiscriminately placed in a wooded area in North Georgia.

I park and we make our way out of the car. Kathy is speechless, eyes wide, but exploring the beautiful architecture. A dark haired gentleman in a dark suit approaches us.

"You must be Katherine – Welcome! My name is James and I'm your director today. Anything you need, please let me know and I'll take care of it for you. Let me show you around."

Kathy is still mute, and frozen in place. I nudge her to respond.

"Um, yes. I'm Katherine. Nice to meet you."

We take a quick tour around the grounds and a few of the buildings. There are a couple that we're not privy to see at this time – per Isaac's request. The chapel and the reception hall. James leads us to the bridal suite. The rooms are stunning in a sea of white linen and lace. Champagne is chilling and an array of hors d'oeuvres are scattered about the rooms.

Our dresses and bags are unloaded from my car and delivered to the suite. Kathy's sister, Sandra, arrives and we begin helping Kathy get dressed. One by one, Gina, Alexandria, and Charlotte arrive in the suite.

At four o'clock, Kathy steps out from her private dressing room and we're stunned silent. The strapless, soft champagne dress hugs every voluptuous curve, flaring at the bottom, in the mermaid style. Her auburn hair is swept up in a chignon, with soft curly tendrils accenting her neck. She is radiant.

Beautiful, stunning, gorgeous, breathtaking – murmurs spread around the room.

"Okay – so I'm guessing one of the wedding colors is black."

We all erupt in laughter, remembering she has no clue about anything occurring today. The five of us are wearing long, black chiffon dresses with an empire waist. Each one with a different style – halter, strapless, asymmetric, V neck, and off the shoulder.

A knock at the door startles us and I go over to answer. A delivery guy has a cart filled with flowers. There are five long stemmed, purple calla lilies tied with purple and black ribbon. Kathy's bouquet consists of purple calla lilies and white roses intermingled. Round at the top, then narrowing to one white rose at the bottom.

"Well, make that black and purple." Kathy acknowledges, as giggles float in the air.

****

The Groom and his Men

"Damn Isaac, you settin' the bar high for all us schmucks coming behind you down the aisle. How the hell did you pull this off?" Patrick asks in disbelief.

"It's all in who you know." Isaac boasts. "Actually, the building that houses the bridal suite and ballroom was damaged in a storm about five years ago. We won the bid to do the repairs and came in under budget. The owner said he owed me big time – so I collected."

"Unbelievable," Leo sighs.

"I called him and he hooked me up with the director. Today was available, so I made a few decisions about colors and such; they've handled the rest. This all-inclusive service is available to anybody."

"Well, I don't know about Katherine, but you impressed the

shit out of me," Edward quips.

"Hey man... Can I speak to you a minute?" I lead Isaac away from the other guys, for some privacy.

"What's up Derek?"

"I hate to bring this up today, but I just found out some news that I thought you would want to know as soon as possible, and I may not have a chance to talk to you until after the honeymoon."

"What's going on?"

"We got word the DA in Memphis has agreed to consolidate the indictment against Rick Foster, so the trial will be held here and not Memphis. Plus, there will only be one trial instead of two."

"Man that's the best news I've heard in a while. Kathy will be relieved. Hopefully, she'll be able to relax on the honeymoon. Oh – what about the motherfucker – is he staying in jail?" Isaac grouses.

"So far. Nobody's posted bail."

"Best place for him. Otherwise, I'm tempted to be judge, jury, and executioner."

****

As the doors open to the chapel, my breath escapes my lungs. It's literally a crystal chapel. The room is enclosed with floor to ceiling windows, giving an enchanting view of the Sun kissing the spectacular colors of Fall for the final time today. Candles along the floor, illuminate the aisle, providing a warm glowing ambiance to the room.

I follow Kathy's sister down the aisle, joining the others at the altar. The men look svelte in their black on black tuxes with purple ties and a purple calla lily for their boutonniere. My Sirs are smoldering and my sex begins to twitch.

The customary bridal march begins and a hush floats across the room. Kathy enters the doorway accompanied by Matt and Ben on each arm.

I want to watch Kathy, but I can't tear my eyes away from Isaac. He is awestruck. I think I could knock him over with a feather. A plethora of emotions appear and fade across his face. The closer she gets, his expression becomes so tender, my heart is bursting.

I blink my eyes quickly, being sure to clarify what I'm seeing. The most fierce and intimidating man I've ever met, has eyes that are glistening in the candlelight.

"Who gives this woman to this man?"

"My brother and I," Ben replies to the wedding officiate.

Yep – the river of tears is flowing.

Derek escorts me, Patrick escorts Kathy's sister Sandra, Gina with Zeke, Alexandria with Leo, and Charlotte and Edward, all make our way back down the aisle.

An absolutely beautiful ceremony shifts into an incredible party in the ballroom. There's a blend of members of Nexus, business associates of Isaac, as well as Kathy's from Atlanta Media. Friends and family members alike.

'All of Me' by John Legend, begins to play and Isaac and Katherine have their first dance. Their first dance turns into a second, as Kathy dedicates "Safe" by Miranda Lambert, to Isaac.

Afterwards, things cut loose with Queen's "Crazy Little Thing Called Love" and the dance party begins. I scan the dance floor and see Mom dancing with someone that I don't know. Dinner, dancing, food, and fun. Everyone seems to be having a great time.

The DJ announces it's time to throw the bouquet. The garter was caught by Zeke, so he is patiently waiting to see whose leg he will be putting it on, after flaunting the fact that he would actually do it.

All of the single ladies, myself included, gather together at the back of the ballroom. Isaac had a smaller replica of Kathy's bouquet made for her to throw. With my height, the chances of me catching it, are slim to none. Kathy takes a look over her shoulder, smiles, turns back around and tosses the bouquet straight into Gina's hands.

The whooping and hollering commences, as Zeke makes his way over to Gina. She plops down in a chair. *After several glasses of champagne, you're not very graceful or ladylike.*

Zeke lifts her dress up her leg until her thigh is exposed. Leo appears out of nowhere, grasping Gina's upper arm, pulling her to her feet.

"Sorry motherfucker – this ain't happening. Not with her," Leo gruffs.

Zeke falls back on his ass, roaring with laughter. "I know that fucker has a thing for Gina. He tries to deny it. I call bull shit," Zeke continues howling with laughter.

Kathy comes over to where we're standing and I take a minute to pick her brain about the wedding. I think she's still a bit in shock. Isaac comes over carrying a thin, rectangular box wrapped in shiny, silver paper with ribbon.

"I think you've been waiting on this," Isaac croons, handing the box to Kathy.

"You said no more gifts," Kathy whines.

"Well, you gave me the gift of a lifetime when you became Mrs. Isaac Jameson, so I had to reciprocate."

Kathy rolls her eyes while she begins unwrapping the box. Isaac reaches over and lights a fire to her ass.

"Don't think I won't bend you over my knee and blister that ass in front of all these people. Roll your eyes at me again…"

"Sorry, Sir," Kathy murmurs her plea for forgiveness.

Her squeals pierce the air when she sees the contents of the box. "Oh my god, we're going to St. Lucia. Oh my god, oh my god, oh my god," she squeals again, jumping into Isaac's arms.

I look around and see all the joy and happiness in this room. But most of all, I see love. Love shared by all walks of life - all ages, all genders, all races.

I look at the two men who surround me. Two men that have brought more love and joy to my life in such a short time, than I've ever known. I've never felt more happy and content in my life.

I think about Mom's advice – *"No one has the right to tell someone their love is wrong"* and *"Don't let your happiness be determined by the opinions of others."*

Our relationship is right for us.

Our love ~ Our way.

DDP

The End

The Nexus Series by Lainie Suzanne

Nexus ~ Book # 1

Katherine Stevens is divorced, with a recently empty nest. She lives a so-called, normal life. With dates few and far between, that she blames on her plump, full figure; Katherine's desires are met vicariously through the characters of her favorite erotic novels.

She is thrust into the erotic world she's always secretly desired, when her best friend arranges a "Girls Night Out" to attend an open house at NEXUS, a local BDSM club. Unbeknownst to her, Katherine catches the eye of the club owner, Master Isaac. He makes her an offer, she can't refuse.

Retired from the Navy, Isaac Jameson took the reins of his family's construction company. With extensive knowledge and training in the BDSM lifestyle, Isaac opened NEXUS; a BDSM club and training center.

The betrayal of his wife and the deception of his former sub, Isaac has sworn off relationships. His play comes only from the training of subs; with no commitment. For years, he's hampered his possessive needs and trust, but this redheaded vixen is taunting his possessive beast within.

Isaac introduces Katherine to her most erotic desires. While caught up in the excitement of her new discoveries, Katherine finds herself vulnerable to evil lurking around her. Will she find strength in her new lifestyle or will it destroy her?

SOLEIL – The Nexus Series #2

Synopsis

Divorced and settled into single life, Debra planned a "Girls Night Out" to rival all, arranging a visit to Nexus, a local BDSM club, for a her best friend Katherine. To their surprise, Katherine catches the eye of the club owner, Isaac, igniting a scorching hot connection that has led to their engagement.

Though she loved her visit to Nexus, Debra has shunned her friend's invitations to become a member, feeling she would be a third wheel to the engaged couple. Then fate intervenes and Debra gets an invitation to Nexus from someone she can't deny.

In her mid-forties, Debra is on the verge of experiencing a life she never realized she desired. Her new found erotic fantasies have her exploring life's most taboo behaviors with not one, but two Alpha males who have stolen her heart. Throwing caution to the wind, Debra embarks on a journey to find love, which could ultimately lead to the destruction of her heart.

Believing she's found the road to happiness, guilt and shame consume her when a tragic loss thrusts her ex-husband back into her life, dredging up regrets of the past.

Will Debra embrace the new life she's discovered at Nexus, or will she allow old feelings and close-minded ideals, to derail her happiness and a chance at love?

DECEIT – The Nexus Series #3

Synopsis

Gina's been drawn to the dark and mysterious Leo, since the moment he first returned to Nexus. However, her sordid past prevents from offering her complete submission.

Leo put up a good fight, but Gina's natural submissiveness taunts his sadistic nature. Leo demands open and honest communication, something Gina struggles with.

Can Gina endure Leo's demanding ways or will her past destroy her and those closest to her, including newlyweds, Katherine and Isaac?

WICKED ~ The Nexus Series #4

CHARLOTTE and EDWARD

You know them.

You envy them.

You secretly crave to be WITH them.

They are WICKED!

Discover the lascivious and tantalizing journey of Charlotte and Edward and how they became the Dynamic Duo of Nexus.

Other publications by Lainie Suzanne

BLOOD MOON ~ An Erotic Vampire Novella

Erotic-Lust ~ Vengeance ~ Immortality

Love fades. Immortality is forever. ~ Unknown

Two years ago, Melaina Harrison's boyfriend was killed in an accident and her life has been in a rut since. Each day merging into the next. Then one fateful night, a dark and seductive stranger walks into her life and shifts her world off its axis. Her new lover's incredible perception of her wants and desires has her reeling in ecstasy; as if he knows her every thought.

Keres Re is beautiful, intelligent, strong; the epitome of the perfect woman. The perfect vampire. Men fall at her feet, both vampire and human. What more could a woman want? Keres wants what all women want, the love of her life. She found her eternal love, however Andrew died in a tragic accident before Keres had a chance to capture his heart for forever. The death she blames on one person – Melaina Harrison.

For two years, Keres has plotted and formulated a plan to avenge the death of her intended eternal lover. She enlists the help of her brother Marco to execute her vengeance.

Will Melaina discover her lover's true existence or will Keres enact her revenge?

About the Author

Lainie Suzanne is from Atlanta, Georgia and makes her home in North Carolina. She's married to her best friend and the love of her life. The mother of four, all flown from the nest, she and her husband share their home with their German Shepherd. She loves sports, listening to music, dancing, spending time with family, and of course...reading.

Find Lainie Suzanne on Social Media:

Facebook
Twitter
Pinterest
Google+
Goodreads
Instagram
Tsu
www.lainiesuzanne.com

www.ingramcontent.com/pod-product-compliance
Lightning Source LLC
Chambersburg PA
CBHW070840120626
46556CB00002B/815